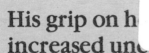

His grip on h increased un...

And Crysten began to wonder if he was trying to turn them into pretzels. "Do you mind?" she said. "I would appreciate it if you would let me go. I am not one of your rolls of linoleum or even a case of rusty nails."

Gregg released her so abruptly she staggered back. "A crabby apple you may be, Crysten, but not a rusty nail," he said, eyeing her appreciatively.

Crysten's rage began to subside. It was no good. She couldn't stay angry at this man for long. The only thing she could do was get away from him as fast as possible and make certain she never saw him again.

She gave him a frosty smile, picked up her bag and left. And wondered at her sense of loss . . .

Kay Gregory is a new author. This book marks her first appearance in the Harlequin Romance line. She is married, lives in Canada and has two grown-up sons.

A Star
for a Ring
Kay Gregory

Harlequin Books

TORONTO • NEW YORK • LONDON
AMSTERDAM • PARIS • SYDNEY • HAMBURG
STOCKHOLM • ATHENS • TOKYO • MILAN

Original hardcover edition published in 1987
by Mills & Boon Limited

ISBN 0-373-02919-5

Harlequin Romance first edition July 1988

CHAPTER ONE

'THERE'S no way they're going to pick *him*,' whispered Crysten.

The woman sitting beside her looked startled. 'Why ever not?'

'Haven't you noticed? They're only choosing attractive women and men with beards today.'

The other woman glanced across the courtroom to the box where eleven selected jury members were already seated, and noted that Crysten was right. Six young women and five bearded men sat, with self-consciously folded hands, staring surreptitiously at the prisoner in the dock. In front of them a tall, powerful-looking man, the one who was unlikely to be picked, stood with arms rigidly at his sides and eyes fixed grimly on the opposite wall.

'I think that's Gregg Malleson,' whispered Crysten's companion.

Beside them uniformed shoulders turned quickly, and authority signalled them to be quiet.

Obeying the signal, Crysten turned her full attention to the man who was now under the probing scrutiny of counsels for the defence and prosecution.

Yes, that was Gregg Malleson, President of Malleson Enterprises, and owner of a chain of building supply outlets which stretched across Western Canada. He was known as one of Vancouver's most high-powered businessmen. The man's physical presence alone was enough to attract attention. His large frame filled a dark three-piece suit in a way which accentuated the powerful shoulders, and seemed to conceal a barely repressed energy which might break out at any moment and command the black-gowned attorneys to damn well make up their minds.

In fact, they only glanced at him for a few seconds before the defence lawyer snapped 'Challenge,' and Gregg Malleson's arms relaxed as he strode confidently back to his seat. It was in the front row of the prospective jurors, a little to Crysten's right. She studied him thoughtfully. Yes, a very nice pair of shoulders. An altogether promising back.

Another beard was selected for the jury, and all those who had not been chosen were thanked for their time and told they could leave.

Crysten rose gratefully, with a murmured goodbye to the woman beside her, and hurried into the bright, plant-lined hallway. That was it, then. She could return to the office and get on with the market research she was doing for Mr Jacobsen.

She had not been particularly pleased when she'd first received the official-looking summons telling her to report to the courthouse for jury duty on September the twentieth. It was a busy time for Getaway Couriers where she worked as assistant to the Vice-President, and she was concerned about keeping on top of her job. But civic duty left her no choice, and in the end her name had not even been called to come forward, so it could have been much worse. She had not been at all anxious to sit in judgement on the soft-eyed young man in the dock, who was accused of assaulting his employer with a three-hole punch in a dispute over the last doughnut in the office food dispenser.

Crysten, still thinking of the prisoner, glanced casually at the man walking beside her—and found herself looking into eyes that were not soft at all, but deep-set, dark and rather fierce. They were studying her with an absorbed concentration which would have been insulting if it had not, at the same time, been totally detached. As though I'm a piece of modern art which he hasn't quite made up his mind about, she thought indignantly. All the same, there was an odd tight feeling in her chest and she felt an almost physical current spark between herself and this rude, annoying and—she couldn't escape it—startlingly attractive man.

'Is there something I can do for you, Mr Malleson?' she asked acidly, as the current flashed and receded. 'Or have I suddenly developed scales? Or a tail? It can't be egg in my hair or jam on my jacket, because I haven't had breakfast yet.'

Her wide, grey eyes fastened on his mouth and she saw the firm, sensuous lips part in an unwilling, slightly rueful smile. It changed his face entirely. In repose it was smooth, strong and austere-looking; a very masculine face. When he smiled it became younger, rakish and quite dazzling in its magnetism. Dark hair waved back from his forehead and curled rebelliously at the base of his neck.

Crysten realised she was staring as rudely as he had been and, reluctantly, she smiled back.

'No.' Gregg Malleson was shaking his head. 'Definitely no scales, and I doubt very much if there's a tail under that very attractive skirt you're wearing.'

Now he was gazing dispassionately at a part of her

anatomy which she considered private. She felt her normally rosy cheeks begin to turn even pinker.

'In that case, I'm not open to view, so if you don't mind . . .' She turned away and started to hurry down the wide, glass-roofed hall towards the exit sign. But her red high heels, which contrasted prettily with the smart black skirt Gregg Malleson had admired, were not made for speedy get-aways, and in a moment she felt a peremptory hand on her arm. His grip was firm, unshakeable and, Crysten was irritated to find, not altogether unpleasant.

She swung round to face him, grey eyes smoking. But before she could open her mouth, he had released her arm, put a proprietorial hand under her elbow and was guiding her through the door.

She found herself in the bright sunlight of a chilly autumn day, staring down the wide white steps which led to the rooftop gardens of Robson Square.

'I apologise.' His tone was all business now. 'I had no right to make personal remarks about your tail.'

Crysten looked at him suspiciously, but his face had a carved granite look about it now. Not even a muscle quivered at the corner of his mouth. He didn't look like the type to poke fun at unknown women, but . . .

'There's no egg in your hair or jam on your jacket, either,' he was continuing, as his eyes studied her appraisingly. 'You said you haven't had breakfast yet. Neither have I.' He glanced at his watch. 'It's nearly noon. Can I make amends by taking you to lunch?'

'No, thank you,' said Crysten quickly. 'I have to get back to work.'

She had no intention of letting this overbearing man think he just had to snap his fingers and offer lunch to have her turn limp with gratitude. Just because he was Gregg Malleson, successful business baron, who had only to lift an eyebrow to have women swooning all over him, didn't mean that she, Crysten Starr, was another of his vapid push-overs.

But when she stole a quick glance at his profile, she saw that his mouth had relaxed and he looked almost relieved. The offer of lunch was only a sop to his conscience, then. The great Gregg Malleson wasn't used to being told off for staring like a star-struck schoolboy. Only she had to admit that he hadn't really looked very star-struck. More like the director of a play, considering a make-over of his leading lady. Well, the maid who brought the tea in the second act, anyway!

She started to move away, but he called after her. 'Wait a minute. If I can't give you lunch, can I drive you somewhere? Do you have far to go?'

She pushed back a strand of light blonde hair which was brushing the corner of her eye. 'No, not far at all. I work for Getaway Couriers just round the corner.'

Now why had she told him that? He hadn't actually asked.

'OK.' He nodded, and smiled politely. Not the dazzling smile she had seen earlier, but a cool, tight-lipped smile which failed to touch his eyes. 'By the way, I didn't imagine you were "open to view" as you put it. You happened to remind me of someone I used to know, that's all. But now I've talked to you, I can see there's no resemblance.'

His tone was non-committal, and Crysten couldn't tell if he was paying her a compliment or telling her that she did not come up to expectations. But the remark explained his earlier scrutiny.

'Really?' she replied, equally non-committal. 'Well, goodbye, Mr Malleson. I expect you have business to attend to as well. Aren't we lucky we weren't chosen for the jury, after all?'

'Very.' His voice was deep, resonant and suddenly quite warm. 'It's been a pleasure. Goodbye, Miss . . .'

'Starr,' Crysten finished for him.

'Appropriate,' he murmured enigmatically.

A moment later he had turned his back on her, and the last she saw of him was his strong, incredibly lithe body running swiftly down the steps to the street. She wondered if he ever walked down stairs, and somehow doubted it.

'Whatever happened to you?' asked her room-mate, Raine, when Crysten arrived home that evening.

'Happened? Nothing.' Crysten threw her bag on the living-room's only easy chair, and stared at her friend in surprise.

'You look as though you've seen a vision, or been hit on the head by a falling fixture—a pink fluorescent one, at that.'

'Oh! All the same, nothing's happened.'

Raine shrugged, tossing her long dark hair over her shoulder. After sharing this apartment with Crysten ever since they had both started work with local companies three years ago, she knew better than to push her. If her friend wanted to talk to her she would, in her own good time. But she couldn't fool Raine that nothing had happened. Crysten was bright, independent and very discreet, but Raine always knew when something was troubling her or, as she suspected was the case this time, when her room-mate was contemplating a new man.

Sometimes Raine knew she was contemplating before Crysten knew it herself. Not that it ever came to anything.

Men liked the happy, self-possessed little blonde with the turned-up nose which was never quite free of freckles. She was bouncy, cheerful and undemanding. But, as far as Raine knew, no one had ever wanted to settle down with her for life. And, to be fair, Crysten had never shown the slightest inclination to settle down herself. She had enjoyed her two years of college and had been happy to start her job with Getaway. Now, as well as working hard during the day, she made time to have dinner with her parents on Sundays, and enjoyed parties, friends and a busy social life which left little opportunity for serious relationships.

Raine sighed. She herself had just become engaged to a young construction worker, and love seemed to her the most wonderful thing in the world. She did wish Crysten could find someone, too. Not that she would dare admit that to her friend, who did not much appreciate this well intentioned interest in her love-life.

'Are you going to be on a jury?' she asked now, feeling almost sure that wouldn't be what had inspired the dreamy look in her room-mate's eye.

'No.' Crysten wandered into the comfortable chaos of their shared bedroom, and peeled off her skirt and jacket. Then she grovelled under the bed and pulled out a pair of faded jeans with white paint streaked down one leg.

'You're not going out tonight,' observed Raine, as Crysten slipped the jeans over her small hips.

'How did you guess? No, as a matter of fact, I'm tired. And it's your turn to make supper.' She tugged on a red

T-shirt and lay back on the sofa, swinging small bare feet across the arm.

Raine looked uncomfortable. 'Yes, I know. But . . .'

'But Bill's taking you out,' finished Crysten, smiling.

'Well—yes. But listen, if you're not too tired, he has a friend . . .'

'No. No friend. You go on. I don't mind a bit.' She leaned her head against the sofa and yawned. 'I'll have TV and a sandwich and an early night. Just what I need.'

Raine saw the visionary look come into her eyes again, and waited.

'Raine?' It was coming. She hadn't had to wait long. 'Mm-hm?'

'What do you know about Gregg Malleson?'

Raine pushed Crysten's bag off the faded red-flowered chair, and sat down slowly. Her room-mate was flying high this time!

'No more than you do, I suppose,' she replied cautiously. 'I read a profile of him in a magazine once. I think he's around thirty-two or three and he has a kid—a boy, if I remember right.'

Crysten's face did not change, but Raine didn't miss the slight stiffening in her friend's shoulders or the way her toes suddenly curled round the arm of the sofa.

'I didn't know he was married.'

Crysten's voice was very casual, and Raine eyed her speculatively. She allowed a few seconds to pass before replying slowly, 'He isn't any more. His wife died some years ago—and I haven't heard that he's exactly pining away from grief, either.'

Neither had Crysten. She had seen numerous pictures of Gregg Malleson on the social pages, attending some charitable function or sporting event with a succession of luscious ladies draped adoringly on his arm.

'Why do you want to know about him?' asked Raine. '*He* wasn't the one on trial, was he?'

'No, of course not. He was called for jury duty—just like I was.'

'Ah, I see. The courts are a great equaliser, aren't they?'

'So's death,' said Crysten dampeningly.

Raine giggled. 'Yes, but you know what I mean. Even *he* couldn't get out of jury duty.'

'I bet he could,' replied Crysten thoughtfully, 'but I don't suppose he tried. It seems to me I've heard that he's quite civic-minded. You know, donations to handicapped athletes, uniforms for kids' baseball teams, that sort of thing.'

'Hm,' sniffed Raine, kicking off her shoes and drawing her legs up on to the chair. 'I thought you said you didn't know much about him.'

'I don't.'

'Oh. Were you talking to him?'

Crysten grinned ruefully. 'If you could call it talking. He made rude remarks about my tail . . .'

'He *what*?'

'Made rude remarks about my tail—and I told him I wasn't open to view.'

Raine shook her head. 'I don't believe it. You meet a man like Gregg Malleson and . . .' She stopped abruptly as the clock Crysten's sister had given them for Christmas began to whirr softly. A moment later, a little wooden cuckoo popped out and reminded them in a fluting, mechanical voice that time was passing by.

'Help,' muttered Raine, jumping up and hurrying into

the bedroom. 'Bill will be here any minute. Are you sure you'll be all right?'

'Yes, of course I am. I'm not sick, you know. Just tired.'

Half an hour later Raine and Bill left in a flurry of laughter and good-natured banter about Crysten's attempt to impersonate Camille, as she lay on the second-hand chintz sofa with her blonde curls spreading over pale green cushions and one well proportioned leg trailed fetchingly on the floor.

As soon as they had gone, Crysten reached for the dial on the TV set. Two game shows, a selection of evening soaps, three comedies which didn't interest her, and a movie she had already seen. She clicked the dial off again and padded into the bathroom. Raine's towel lay over the edge of the bath. She pushed it aside. Yes, as she had thought, her book was underneath it, slightly damp but still readable. She picked it up, wandered into the kitchen, and made herself a cheese and pickle sandwich. Then she subsided on to the couch again, clutching book, sandwich and a glass of milk in a precarious balancing act. The operation was accomplished successfully with only a few drops spilled on to her old red T-shirt.

It had certainly been quite a day. What with courtrooms, the usual dramas at the office—and Gregg Malleson. . .

Crysten closed her eyes and saw again the tall, athletic body and the intense dark eyes which had stared at her so unswervingly from under those thick black brows. She wondered about the woman whose resemblance to herself had been so engrossing.

At the back of her mind, a vague, distressing memory stirred. In a way, it had been there all along. Her immediate reaction to Gregg Malleson had been one of fascination, but almost as quickly had come a faint, disturbing feeling that there was something unlikeable about this man. Not just his arrogant self-confidence, but something else. Something that had happened a long time ago.

She shook her head and shifted restlessly on the sofa. It didn't matter, anyway. She was not likely to meet him again. He had materialised like the ghost of some forgotten ancestor—or lover—and vanished again just as quickly. And that was the last she would see of the President of Malleson Enterprises.

She picked up her book and began to flip through the pages. For some reason she found it hard to concentrate. It wasn't a very good book, anyway.

She was about to wander into the kitchen to see what else there was to eat, when the doorbell rang.

Damn! She didn't want visitors now. Irritably she pattered over to the door.

'Good evening,' said Gregg Malleson, looking down at her from what seemed to be a great height. He raised black eyebrows expressively and gave her a brief smile. 'Good grief, you're even smaller than I remembered!'

Crysten took a step backwards and drew in her breath.

'That's because I had heels on.' She frowned. Why was she bothering to explain her height? 'What on earth are you doing here?' she demanded, recovering her senses and raising her chin indignantly.

'I'm not at all sure myself. I told you you reminded me of someone.' The handsome mouth twisted wryly. 'But that memory is better forgotten. Anyway, I thought that perhaps since you couldn't manage lunch today, you might be free for dinner. So I asked your Mr Jacobsen where I could track you down. He's an old acquaintance of mine.'

'Yes, Mallesons is one of our accounts, isn't it?' said Crysten vaguely, still holding on to the door as though he might try to storm the barricades of number 2A, Chaffinch Apartments.

Gregg nodded. 'That's right, it is. For the moment, anyway. We've had some problems with you people lately. Can I come in?'

She held the door open another six inches, and saw a gleam of amusement in his eyes.

'I don't ravish innocent maidens before dinner,' he informed her in that slow, deep voice which seemed to curl around her like warm molasses. For one ridiculous moment, she felt like asking him how he knew she was an innocent maiden, and telling him that it was after *her* dinner.

'Of course. Do come in.' She stepped back haughtily, holding her head high and trying to look dignified. It worked quite well until she remembered the paint on her blue jeans and saw him staring interestedly at the milk stain on her T-shirt.

'What's the matter?' she asked defensively, trying to hold her book casually over the stain.

'Not a thing.' He sauntered over to the sofa with a smile which she was sure held a hint of mockery in it. 'May I sit down?'

'Of course.'

He lowered himself smoothly on to the cushions and pushed aside the jumble sale coffee-table to stretch long legs in front on him.

'Well?' said Crysten, still holding the book in front of her like a shield,

'Well, what?'

'What did you come here for?'

'I told you. To take you out to dinner.'

'Why? Anyway, I've already eaten.'·

'So I see,' he replied, eyes straying pointedly to the area of the stain. 'And for heaven's sake, put that book down! It's not hiding a thing.'

Crysten opened her mouth to tell him he could leave right now, then shut it again and put her hands on her hips. She glared at him, for once in her life quite speechless. If Raine could see her now she wouldn't believe it!

'You, you . . .' She tried to get out the words that would tell this impossible man, in very expressive terms, just exactly what she thought of arrogant, self-satisfied jerks who didn't have the courtesy to ignore things like spotted T-shirts. And paint-splattered jeans, she added to herself, as she saw his eyes wander thoughtfully down her legs.

Then she noticed his lips quiver as his mouth quirked up at the corners. She stared at him, and her fury subsided as quickly as it had arisen. She supposed she did look funny, trying to act the duchess in clothes better suited to a deplorably grubby kitchen maid. She felt laughter begin to bubble in her throat.

'Is it a good book?' he enquired soothingly, when he saw her eyes light up with unaffected self-mockery.

'No, not very,' she admitted, chuckling, as she sank into the chair across from him. 'It's just one long sex scene after another, with occasional interruptions for tea and toast and trips to the bathroom.'

His lips twitched. 'Sounds wonderful.' He regarded her speculatively from under heavy lids. 'On second thoughts, maybe we *shouldn't* go out.'

'Forget it,' grinned Crysten.

Gregg sighed and raised his eyes to the ceiling. 'Ah, well, if you insist,' he said in tones of deep resignation. 'Dinner it is, then.'

'But I told you, I've already eaten.'

'Nonsense.' He gestured to the empty plate lying on the coffee-table. 'You can't call that a meal. From the looks of it, all you've had is something unpleasant with pickles.'

'Cheese. And it wasn't unpleasant.'

'It certainly wasn't a meal. Go and change.'

'Now, wait a minute! Who do you think you're ordering . . .'

'Don't quarrel with me, Miss Starr. You *haven't* eaten, and I'd like to take you out.' He uncoiled his long body from the sofa and came towards her.

A moment later he had pulled her to her feet. They were standing very close together and her hands were still in his. For a second their eyes locked. Something jolted in Crysten's stomach and there was a strange, weak sensation in her legs.

'Go on,' he said softly, releasing her hands and giving her a little shove towards the bedroom. 'I'm getting hungry.'

Crysten had to admit that she was hungry, too. All the same, she wasn't at all sure why she was allowing this overpowering male to push her into going out with him. Raine would have said it wasn't like her at all. But there was something very persuasive about Gregg Malleson. She shook her head. What was it she ought to remember about him?

She paused with her favourite blue dress half-way over her head. There *was* something. Gregg was not all he seemed, she was sure of it. Although what he seemed was bad enough, she thought irritably as she tried to catch the zipper at the back of her dress and missed. He was over-bearing, over-confident, smug and ... She sighed. Altogether fascinating.

Vaguely, as she finally caught up with the zipper, she wondered why he was bothering with her. She was hardly in the same class as the ladies with whom he was photographed in the papers. She shrugged. Perhaps she was just a change of pace. She reminded him of someone from his past and he was curious about her. Or else he was just not used to being turned down, and wanted to prove to himself that he could add her to his collection as easily as he had every other woman who happened to attract his attention. Not that it mattered to her. The day which had begun with a panic-stricken sprint to the courthouse because she had forgotten to get out of bed was about to end on an equally unusual note.

And that would be all there was to it, she told herself firmly, as she dabbed cologne behind her ears, slipped into her highest heels and went to join Gregg in the living-room.

He was waiting for her by the door, his shoulder resting easily against the wall.

'Wow!' He whistled approvingly. 'Blue was obviously made for you, Miss Starr. Or perhaps you were made for blue.'

'Thank you.' She looked away, feeling ridiculously pleased, even though she knew he was probably used to paying extravagant compliments. Then she glanced back at him, as a sudden thought occurred to her. 'You don't even know my name, do you, Mr Malleson?' She smiled, a teasing gleam in her eye.

He grinned, a little sheepishly. 'Well, as a matter of fact,' he admitted, 'I forgot to ask Mark Jacobsen. I thought of you as Star.'

'It's Crysten,' she informed him, remembering that she intended to have words with Mr Jacobsen in the morning. 'And it's Starr with two Rs.'

'Is it?' he said, smiling down at her. 'I like it better with one.' He touched the back of his hand very lightly against her cheek. 'And I'm Gregg with two Gs.' He opened the door into the hall.

A light green Rover 2000 was pulled up against the kerb. Gregg helped her into the passenger seat and swung himself in beside her.

He drove quickly down Georgia Street and soon they were passing Lost Lagoon, with its fountain throwing plumes of rainbow-coloured magic at the night. Then they were high above the waters of Burrard Inlet, and far below them a small boat winked at them through the darkness. Across the Lion's Gate Bridge the black shapes of the North Shore mountains would have been invisible but for a line of lights trailing like Christmas chains beside the ski-lift.

Half an hour later they were seated in the window of a small, wood-panelled restaurant on a hillside overlooking the water, and the lights of the city gleamed fairylike in the reflecting depths of the harbour.

'It's beautiful,' whispered Crysten.

'Yes.' Gregg was not looking at the lights on the water, but at the far softer light that was shining in her eyes.

After a time the waiter brought champagne, and Gregg ordered salad and lobster, and a dessert so smooth it melted in her mouth. They spoke lightly of the view from the window, and the problems of driving in

Vancouver traffic and what they liked to eat. Gregg was a steak and lobster man, and Crysten favoured exotic casseroles. But when they had finished, all Crysten really knew about Gregg Malleson was that he was the active and energetic president of Mallesons who had taken over the family business when his father had retired seven years ago. And that she had known already.

'All right?' he asked, when the final plate had been discreetly taken away, and they sat relaxed in the dimness, over coffee filled with cream and brandy.

'Wonderful.' Gregg could just see the gentle curve of her lips. He reached a finger across the table and slowly traced the outline of her mouth. His eyes looked very deep in the half-light.

'I'm glad.' His smile was warm and his finger moved unhurriedly down her cheek.

Crysten felt a deep, slow warmth envelop her. She leaned back in her chair and sighed softly.

Suddenly a waiter dropped a spoon, somebody snapped an angry reprimand—and something flickered in Crysten's brain. That woman she resembled, surely . . . No, the memory would not come. She shook her head and the spell was broken.

'What's the matter?' asked Gregg, his eyes concerned.

'Nothing. I don't know. I can't . . . It's just . . .' She knew she was babbling and took a deep breath. This evening must be brought back to common sense and reality—fast.

'What was it you said about having trouble with Getaway lately?' she asked brightly, casting about for something to say and suddenly recalling his earlier remark. She had meant to ask what he was talking about at the time.

The concern in his eyes faded and was replaced by irritation. The look he gave her now was reserved, unemotional, and he had become the tough executive again with no time for the inefficiencies and mistakes of others.

'I haven't said anything much about it—yet,' he replied ominously. 'But if any more of my documents arrive two days late I'll have plenty to say. In the right quarters, though.'

'Sometimes I am the right quarters,' replied Crysten coolly, resenting the implication that she was just a junior employee with no authority to handle problems.

'I doubt it.' His mouth had tightened slightly. Then slowly he relaxed and smiled at her, a quiet, almost formal smile. 'Don't worry, Crysten,' he said lightly. 'There's no need for you to trouble your head about it.'

'My empty little head, you mean,' said Crysten with icy sweetness.

'Don't be difficult. All I meant was that if the problems continue, I shall take steps to solve them, and it has nothing whatever to do with you. I'm quite sure *you* haven't been sabotaging my deliveries. So let's leave it, shall we, and talk about something else?' He leaned back in his chair with the complacent boardroom smile of a chairman who knows he has the upper hand.

Crysten felt her temper begin to rise. Why did Gregg do this to her? She had only met him this morning, and ever since then she seemed to have been in a state of semi-permanent fury.

'I don't want to talk about something else,' she said now, spots of indignant colour appearing on her cheeks. 'You just said the company I work for has messed you up. I'm Mr Jacobsen's assistant, and I'd like to know why.'

'Why you're Mr Jacobsen's assistant?' He raised his eyebrows enquiringly. 'Probably because you have a pretty face.' He was being deliberately provocative and Crysten knew it. All the same, the provocation was effective.

'That's totally irrelevant,' she snapped, almost stamping her feet.

'Oh, I wouldn't say that.' Gregg regarded her lazily, from under half-closed lids, and Crysten, with a strong suspicion he was trying to incite her to violence, gripped her coffee-cup tightly and resisted an urge to pour the contents over his head.

'I'll speak to Mr Jacobsen tomorrow,' she told him, in a voice which she fought desperately to keep calm, efficient and devoid of emotion. 'I'm sure you'll find there was an excellent reason for the delays.'

'I'm sure I will.' Gregg's voice was equally calm. 'Fog's always a good excuse.'

'Hardly an excuse.' Crysten smiled frostily, refusing to be baited. 'Planes don't take off in fog, and in case you haven't noticed it's September. Vancouver does occasionally get fog at this time of year.'

'Apparently.' Gregg sounded bored. He made a discreet signal, and a moment later the waiter arrived with the bill.

His hands lingered on the back of her neck as he helped her on with her coat. She shivered, although it wasn't cold, and hurried away from him towards the car park.

The drive home was silent. Crysten was fuming, and not at all sure what had happened to this evening, which had started with TV and a sandwich, progressed to a romantic candlelight dinner, and now seemed to have degenerated into the aftermath of a quite unnecessary battle. A thoroughly silly battle, too. She was very conscious of the man beside her in the car. She watched his strong hands controlling the wheel, and remembered how they had felt against her neck. She wasn't being honest with herself, either. She knew quite well what had happened to the evening. She was attracted, quite alarmingly attracted, to this man. But the moment he had attempted to come close to her she had adopted that brittle, distant attitude which immediately turned him into a patronising tycoon who reduced her to bubble-headed idiocy.

What was it that made her shy away from him? She just didn't know—or couldn't remember.

She shook her fair curls briskly and turned to stare through the window. They were crossing the Lion's Gate Bridge again and the world was very far away. As they pulled into Stanley Park, Crysten lifted her eyes from the shadowy branches of the trees brushing past the car, and stole a look at Gregg's profile. He was staring straight ahead at the road, the strong lines of his nose and jaw outlined against the moonlight. Crysten resisted a sudden urge to touch him.

'Thank you for the dinner. I enjoyed it,' she murmured, in a small, placating voice.

His head did not move, but she saw the muscles in his face tighten.

'Good. I'm glad.' The deep voice was withdrawn, polite—and extraordinarily attractive.

'Will you come in?' she asked doubtfully when the car pulled up outside Chaffinch Apartments.

'No, it's late. I'll see you to the door.'

She fumbled for her key, feeling his nearness and his

eyes on her back as he waited behind her on the steps. She continued her fruitless search for the key.

A minute passed. She was still fumbling. Suddenly she could feel Gregg's warm breath on her neck. Startled, she stared up at him, one hand still clutching her bag, the other gripping the handle of the door.

'For God's sake,' he muttered. 'Here, give it to me.'

He took the bag from her, unzipped a pocket, and handed her a ring of keys.

'How did you know they were there?' she gasped.

'I saw you put them there. Now close your mouth.'

Crysten realised she was gaping up at him like a beached beluga. She snapped her mouth shut quickly, and Gregg smiled. It was a smile that sent her pulses racing.

She turned quickly to the door, keys now clutched securely in her hand.

'Don't run away. At least let me say goodbye.' His voice was gentle now, caressing and impossibly persuasive. She felt his hands on her shoulders as he turned her slowly to face him. They were still on her shoulders when she put her own hands against his chest to push him away—and when he bent his head to kiss her, quickly and soundly, on the lips.

CHAPTER TWO

FOR a moment the world turned upside down. A hundred warning signals flashed through Crysten's head—and were ignored. Her fingers began to move across Gregg's chest, and she could feel the muscles beneath his shirt. His kiss was firm and warm and gentle. She heard the sound of indrawn breath, and knew it was her own and that she must stop this, now, before it was too late.

But when Gregg released her shoulders and held her away from him it was already too late to hide the turmoil seething through her body. She stood, unable to move, rooted to the step and staring up at him. Her big, grey eyes were wide and startled. Then slowly her breathing returned to normal.

'You, I . . .' she began, groping frantically for her keys again, and finding she had dropped them. She bent to pick them up, but Gregg was quicker.

'You should take better care of these,' he smiled, as he handed them to her. 'I'm amazed you ever manage to get into your apartment.' He seemed completely unaffected by the kiss which had thrown her into such agitation.

'That's not fair,' she murmured, taking the keys and inserting the wrong one quickly in the lock. 'Damn,' she added, as she finally got it right. 'You know that's not fair. You distracted me.'

'Did I? I'm glad. You didn't seem to mind, though.'

She glanced at him quickly, and saw that his dark head was bent towards her and that he was watching her with a slow, speculative smile on the lips which a moment ago had been pressed against her own.

She looked away. 'You took me by surprise.'

'I know. Don't you like surprises? I thought you were angry with me, so I figured we might as well part on a friendlier note.'

Crysten felt her temper beginning to boil again. The arrogance of the man! Did he really think that all he had to do was give her a quick kiss and she would melt like butter to his charms? But she had melted, hadn't she? And he knew it.

She turned away from him and pushed open the door. 'Thank you for the evening, Mr Malleson.' She tossed the formal words at him over her shoulder. 'It was very interesting.'

'I thought so, too.' She thought she detected a hint of laughter in his voice. 'I enjoyed it. Goodnight, Star.'

Just before she pushed the door closed behind her, she felt the very light touch of fingers on her cheek. Then the door slammed and she was alone in the empty apartment.

'Damn,' she muttered to herself, and then, reverting to a phrase out of her childhood, 'Double damn.' She switched on the light, kicked her shoes across the room and stumbled into the bedroom.

'What's the matter?' asked Raine, coming in a few minutes later.

'Nothing. Nothing's the matter,' she snapped, thumping herself down on the edge of her bed and beginning to peel off her tights.

'Oh, is that why you look like a thundercloud on a sunny day?' replied Raine, serenely unruffled in her rosy, love-filled world.

Crysten gave her a watery smile. She rarely snapped at Raine, and it didn't feel right. 'I'm sorry. It's just that I changed my mind and went out this evening.'

'I can see that. From the look on your face, I'd say you should have stuck with your original decision. TV and a sandwich might have done more for your disposition.'

'Yes, they might at that. I went out with Gregg Malleson.'

'Well!' Raine raised her eyebrows and pursed her lips in a soundless whistle. Then, seeing Crysten still scowling at the wall, she added sympathetically, 'Is he a real bastard, then?'

Crysten sighed. 'No. At least, that's the trouble ... I don't know. He's used to having his own way, I think. But he was very nice at the beginning of the evening. Then he started acting as if I was some bird-brained idiot with more looks than sense.' She pulled a nightgown from underneath her pillow and put it on back to front.

Raine grinned. 'Sometimes you are,' she remarked without malice. 'What did you do to stir him up?' Raine knew her friend well.

'Nothing, really. We were getting along just fine, and then I asked him why he wasn't happy with Getaway's service.'

'And you picked the wrong time to ask,' finished Raine.

'Yes, I suppose I did, but ... Oh, Raine—he's so—I don't know. He's attractive, but something about him scares me off. I don't even know what it is, apart from the obvious things ...'

'Such as?'

'Oh, such as being overbearing and opinionated and arrogant ...'

'And sexy and irresistible and you like him very much!' Raine was laughing at her.

'Yes, I guess I do—some of the time.' She shrugged. 'Oh, well, it doesn't matter. I won't see him again, anyway.'

'Are you sure?'

'Quite sure.'

'Hmm.' Raine stared at her friend perceptively, but said no more.

Would she see him again? wondered Crysten, as she lay in bed later, unable to sleep and trying not to think about what she would look like in the morning with bags under her eyes and a mouth that kept wanting to yawn.

It wasn't very likely. She supposed the only reason he had kissed her was to prove that he could make her respond. And he had proved it. Anyway, it was over. Episode finished and closed. She wouldn't waste time thinking about it any more. She wouldn't even tell Mr Jacobsen about Gregg's delivery problems with Getaway. Mighty Malleson could look after his affairs without her help! As, no doubt, he would. She would certainly have words with Mr Jacobsen about giving out her address, though.

She turned over, closed her eyes and pulled the pillow over her head. . . . When he had said goodnight, he had called her Star . . .

It took her two hours to get to sleep.

When Crysten saw Mr Jacobsen in the morning, the first thing she said to him was, 'Please don't give my address to anyone again.'

But kindly Mr Jacobsen, eyes twinkling in a round, cherubic face, only laughed and told her that she might do a lot worse than Gregg Malleson.

'That may be so,' replied Crysten sourly, 'but it just happens that I don't want to "do" anyone.'

Mr Jacobsen shook his head and suggested that in that case, perhaps she would reply to the stack of complaints on his desk occasioned by the recent spell of fog.

Sifting through the pile of acrimonious letters and the telephone messages which had blasted the ears off blameless receptionists, Crysten reflected for at least the two-hundredth time that the public was very unreasonable. Much as Getaway would have liked the ability to perform miracles, there was no way they could wave a magic wand to waft away fog, snow, bomb scares and engine trouble. But some of their clients expected just that. Gregg Malleson, for instance.

In the bright, brisk light of morning, surrounded by letters, financial statements and ringing telephones, the events of last night seemed strangely unreal. Crysten wondered if she had succumbed to an attack of temporary insanity. But she was over it now. She wouldn't hear from Gregg again, and even if she did she would not go out with him. Only trouble, heartache and further disruption of her sanity lay in that direction. She remembered the glamorous ladies in the photographs, and her resolve was strengthened.

All the same, for the first few days after that memorable evening, every time the phone rang she was the first to grab it. Raine watched her pensively, but said nothing. Usually it turned out the calls were Bill wanting to murmur sweet nothings in Raine's ear, or John inviting Crysten to a hockey game.

The mad dashes to the telephone table began to taper off.

She went to the hockey game with John, who was an old friend on the rebound from a broken engagement, and once she went dancing with Roger from Sales, which quickly turned out to be a mistake. Dancing was not really what Roger had in mind, and Crysten did not have Roger in mind for the kind of activity he wanted.

By the end of a week, the memory of Gregg was fading fast. Occasionally Raine would notice Crysten gazing with a surprisingly rapt expression at the neighbours putting out rubbish or cleaning windows, but these periods of abstraction only lasted a few seconds. When, after a hectic weekend spent helping friends paint their house, a paint-streaked Crysten bounced cheerfully into the apartment one evening and announced that it had been a wonderful day, Raine was sure that her friend had completely recovered from her unusual moodiness. The grumpy, confused young woman of a week ago had gone, and in her place was the breezy, easy-going companion Raine was used to.

On Monday morning, Mr Jacobsen stamped into Crysten's office with his cherub's mouth turned down in a disgruntled grimace.

'What's this all about?' he demanded, thrusting a crumpled-looking letter under her nose.

Crysten took it from him and read it through quickly. It was signed by Gregg Malleson and was a short, badly spelt, but very precise letter, informing Getaway that unless they pulled up their socks and managed to get important documents to their destinations on time and intact from now on, Mallesons would be cancelling their contract. Apparently the final straw had been a tender to provide materials for a new hotel in Winnipeg which had arrived too late for the deadline. After the signature there was a postscript, which added,

'I was under the impression that Miss Starr of your office would look into my concerns with a view to improving the service.'

Crysten looked up to find Mr Jacobsen's eyes fixed on her face, and his eyebrows raised in enquiry.

'Well?' he asked.

'Er—yes,' murmured Crysten, wondering why her heart was thumping so oddly. 'I don't know anything about this last complaint, but I suppose it's true that I said I'd look into his concerns. Only he'd already told me not to bother my head about it, so I decided to take him at his word.'

Mr Jacobsen's eyebrows came down quickly and she saw his mouth turn up at the corners.

'Your *pretty* little head?' he asked innocently.

Crysten was forced to smile. 'Yes, I guess that's exactly what he meant.'

'Aha!' Mr Jacobsen pulled thoughtfully at his lip. 'Well, in view of Mr Malleson's dissatisfaction, I think we'd better send someone to see him. And since he mentioned "Miss Starr of your office", I think it had better be you.'

Colour flooded her cheeks. 'Me?' she repeated, her voice coming out in a strangled squeak. 'But I don't think Mr Malleson—I mean, Roger from Sales . . .'

'No, I think Crysten from the Vice President's office would have a much more pacifying effect.' Mr Jacobsen's eyes were bright, kindly—and determined.

'Yes, of course, if you want me to.' She picked up a paper knife and stabbed it into her blotter.

'Right, then. You set up an appointment as soon as you can. Get back to me when you've seen him.'

Crysten nodded, waited for him to go, and then picked up the phone quickly, without giving herself time to think. 'I'd like to speak to Mr Malleson's secretary, please,' she said briskly, when her call was finally answered.

'One minute, please.' The receptionist sounded bored, and a moment later Crysten was cut off.

She dialled again, repeated her request and pointed out that she had already been cut off once.

'Oh, have you? That's too bad.' The receptionist was obviously not interested, and by the time Crysten was connected to Gregg's secretary, she was fuming.

Her mood was not much better when, later that afternoon, she walked through the doors of the local outlet of Malleson Enterprises, and said she had an appointment with Mr Malleson.

'Oh, yes,' said the bald-headed man in charge of the store. 'He's around somewhere. Doubt if he's in his office, though. Try the warehouse.'

'Thanks,' replied Crysten as the man waved her to the rear of the building and told her to go out the back. She followed his instructions, then paused to look about her.

Where she stood, the warehouse was cavernous and dimly lit. There didn't seem to be anyone around. But in the distance, where huge doors opened on to a loading dock, the sun shone brightly on a group of men who were heaving large objects on to an oversized truck.

Crysten walked slowly towards them. At first, she couldn't distinguish one figure from another because the sun was in her eyes. Then she heard a familiar voice shout 'Steve', and the sudden lurch in her chest surprised her.

'Steve,' the voice bellowed again. 'Where the hell do you think you're going with that forklift?'

As Crysten approached the group by the doors, she saw a wiry little man jump down on to the concrete after backing the forklift towards a tall figure standing beside the truck.

The figure was Gregg Malleson, but not the well dressed executive she had met in the courthouse. This Gregg was taller and more massive than she remembered. His striped business shirt was open at the neck, and on one shoulder he was balancing a heavy roll of something which was probably linoleum. The dark hair was dishevelled now, and sweat glistened on his brow. She could see the muscles straining against the fabric of his shirt. As she came up to him, he threw the linoleum easily on to the truck and turned to face her, pulling out a handkerchief to mop his face.

'Good afternoon,' said Crysten, trying not to stare too hard at this giant of a man who, for a moment, had made her feel insignificant and vulnerable.

'Good afternoon,' he replied carelessly. 'What are you doing here?'

She stopped feeling insignificant and felt indignant instead.

'I have an appointment with you. At three o'clock.' She glanced pointedly at her watch, which said five minutes past three.

'Oh, have you?' He wiped the handkerchief around his neck and shoved it into his pocket. 'What for?'

She gave an exasperated sigh. 'Because you wrote to Mr Jacobsen and complained—and because *you* men-

tioned my name.' The last words came out sputtering like
a firework about to detonate.

'Ah, yes.' Gregg grinned suddenly. 'I did, didn't I?
Sheila told me someone was coming at three. I guess I
forgot the time.'

'You forgot the appointment, you mean,' said Crysten
tartly. But she was beginning to smile herself. His change
of mood was infectious.

'OK. Come on.' He took her arm and started to
shepherd her out of the warehouse. 'We'll talk in my
office.'

Crysten was startled by the jolt that went through her
at the simple touch of his hand on her elbow.

He led her through the store, where the bald-headed
man nodded at them, and up a flight of stairs. A tall,
young receptionist sat at a desk, busily munching
crackers. In front of Gregg's office, which was large,
cluttered and in need of paint, a grey-haired woman was
typing a letter.

'Sheila, this is Crysten Starr from Getaway Couriers,'
said Gregg. 'She tells me I forgot her appointment.'

'Which you did,' replied Sheila, eyeing him severely
over her glasses. 'Mr Malleson is *not* reliable about
appointments, Miss Starr. I think he forgets them on
purpose.'

'I don't.' Gregg was grinning at her, not at all put out
by her censure.

'Yes, you do, Mr Malleson. You know you're much
happier heaving bales about in the warehouse and
shouting at the shippers than you are dealing with
statements and pricing and taxes—and the manager
who's just resigned in Calgary.'

Gregg raised his eyebrows. 'Has he resigned again?'

'He has. Because you didn't get around to authorising his expense sheet.'

'All right, all right, I'll get to it and I'll calm him down,' Gregg assured her. He turned to Crysten. 'Come on, let's escape from this dragon-lady and go into my office. Sheila thinks I'm beyond redemption.'

'Huh! Don't let him fool you, Miss Starr,' Sheila called after them. 'He may ignore the details, but nothing important gets by him. Ever.'

Crysten had no difficulty in believing her.

'So I'm a detail and not specially important,' she remarked drily, as Gregg pulled out a chair for her and sat down behind the desk, his long legs stretched in front of him and his hands folded casually behind his head. She found herself staring at the strong sinews of his neck.

'Not at all.' His reply to her barb came promptly. 'I just got involved, that's all. But I hoped Mark would send you. That's why I wrote the letter.'

Crysten half rose from her chair, then sat down again.

'Did you say that's why you wrote . . .'

'The letter. That's right.'

'But—I don't understand. Do you mean to say that tender was actually delivered on time?'

Just for a moment Gregg's eyes hardened and Crysten had another glimpse of the tyrant she had seen shouting at his workers in the warehouse. Then the lines of his face relaxed. But his reply was terse.

'No. It most certainly was *not* on time! We lost a good deal of money over that one. But normally I handle that sort of thing by phone. It's quicker.'

She had no doubt that speed and getting things done 'now' had always been the determining factors in Gregg's business dealings.

'Also, you can't spell,' she remarked sweetly, trying not to laugh when she saw the startled indignation in his eyes. 'Phoning gets round that problem, doesn't it?'

Gregg removed his hands from behind his head, leaned forward and rested them on the desk. His intense eyes fastened on her face and showed no sign of amusement at first. Then slowly his mouth broke into a grin and his eyes lit with laughter.

'Nice one,' he replied, looking at her with something like admiration. 'You're right. I can't. Only usually no one has the bad manners to say so.'

'The nerve, you mean. You can be quite intimidating.'

'I know. It's very useful.' He was still grinning at her.

'I'm sure it is.' Crysten found herself grinning back. 'Incidentally, why don't you ask Sheila to fix up your spelling for you—on those rare occasions when you don't use the phone?'

'She does, I suppose,' he replied off-handedly. 'She was away when I wrote that letter to Mark Jacobsen though, so Doris, our receptionist, typed it up for me. I guess she can't spell, either.'

'I guess not.' Crysten's tone was abstracted. She still had not got to the bottom of Gregg's odd remark that he had written the letter because he hoped Mr Jacobsen would send her to see him.

'All right,' she said, smoothing her grey skirt and becoming businesslike. 'I don't see why you couldn't have phoned me if you wanted me to handle your problem . . .'

'I didn't give a damn who handled my problem—as long as someone did. I wanted to see you again, that's all.'

'To see me?' Crysten was mystified. 'Then why didn't you ask me?'

'I didn't think you'd come,' he replied simply.

Crysten, looking into his eyes, deep-set and dark in the brightness of the room, saw that his doubt was genuine. So even Gregg Malleson was not always sure of his power to get what he wanted. Besides, he had guessed right. She *had* decided that if he called her she would refuse to see him. At the moment, with his powerful presence so close to her across the desk, she could not even remember why she had wanted to refuse.

She took a deep breath. This was not the time to think about her feelings for Gregg. She was here on company business and on her employer's time.

'I expect you were right,' she said firmly. 'I probably wouldn't have come. Now, let's get down to the facts about your tender.'

Gregg straightened his long body so that it was further away from her. 'OK,' he replied flatly. 'Let's do that.'

In a calm, impassive voice, he proceeded to give the precise details of shipment dates, way-bill numbers, destinations and arrival times. In two cases, the late delivery was due strictly to fog. In the case of the Winnipeg tender, Crysten was beginning to get a strong hunch that she knew exactly what had happened.

In a voice as emotionless as his, she suggested he check his copy of the way-bill for destination, address and date of shipment.

Gregg shook his head impatiently, but he did as she asked and shouted for Sheila to bring him the way-bill. They waited in a slightly strained silence, during which Gregg pretended to be reading something important on his desk and Crysten stared at the spots on the wall and thought of the improvements a can of paint would make. That was probably one of the details Gregg ignored.

A few minutes later Sheila came in looking flustered.

'We can't find it,' she apologised. 'Doris says she sent the tender, but she seems to have lost the file copy.'

'Blast!' muttered Gregg. Then in a voice which could have lifted the roof, he roared, 'Doris!'

Doris scuttled in, looking scared but defiant. Crysten thought she might have looked the same if *she* had been the target of Gregg's wrath.

'What do you mean, you lost it?' he thundered, eyebrows drawn together in a fierce scowl.

'I'll look again,' the girl muttered quickly, as she almost ran out of his office.

Sheila shook her head. 'It's hopeless,' she murmured. 'Doris just doesn't care since she gave notice. She's leaving in two weeks, you know.'

'Is she? I'd forgotten.' Gregg's head was bent over his desk and Crysten couldn't see his face, but from his voice she concluded that Doris's future was of no great interest to him.

Five minutes passed, and eventually Doris reappeared with her mouth turned down in a sulky pout. Silently she handed a rumpled way-bill to Gregg.

'Give it to Miss Starr.' He waved her away and gestured peremptorily at Crysten.

'Thank you,' said Crysten, carefully inspecting the paper. It was as she had suspected. The address on the way-bill was not the address Gregg had given her, nor had the package been dispatched on the date Gregg had mentioned. Doris, in her lack of concern for a job she was about to leave, had sent it one day late and to the wrong address.

'I'll fire her,' muttered Gregg, when Crysten had

explained the confusion.

'You can't, she's already quit,' objected Sheila. 'Not that you would anyway, once you'd simmered down,' she added over her shoulder as she left the office.

'I bloody well would if she didn't shape up!' Gregg shouted after her.

Crysten thought he probably would. His bark might be a lot noisier than his bite, but she couldn't see this human dynamo putting up with inefficiency for long.

'Well, Miss Starr, I apologise. And I was quite wrong about your head.'

'What?' Crysten gaped at him, wondering what on earth he was talking about.

He grinned. 'It's not only pretty. It's also intelligent and capable. And I'm afraid Mallesons was entirely to blame for this mess. I'm very impressed with you, Crysten Starr.'

He stood up and came round the desk towards her. Feeling at a disadvantage with this giant of a man towering over her, Crysten jumped hastily to her feet.

'Thank you,' she replied formally. 'I'm glad we solved the problem.'

'So am I.' He was standing very close to her now, and long fingers curved slowly round the back of her neck, drawing her towards him. She started to pull away, and then found her legs would not move. He bent his head, and sensuous lips closed firmly over hers. She felt her body tremble. His kiss was gentle at first, then harder, more demanding. Once again the world slid away from beneath her feet as his hands moved down her back and pulled her so close against him that she could feel the beating of his heart. His caress was deliberate, very sensual, and the sensations pounding through her body were like nothing she had ever known before. When he let her go she realised that her own arms were around his neck. Slowly he unclasped them and held her hands against his chest.

'Well, Star?' There was a small smile on his lips and his eyebrows were raised in quizzical enquiry.

'Why did you do that?' she whispered, trying desperately to regain control of her head, which seemed to be revolving in multi-coloured circles.

'I wanted to make sure that what I remembered was really true.' His voice was even deeper than she had thought.

'What did you remember?'

'That your lips tasted like apples on a fresh spring morning.' He still held her hands against his chest and his eyes were smiling at her.

'You must mean crab-apples,' she said breathlessly, afraid of what this man was doing to her, and fighting to break the spell.

'You're an impossible woman.' He laughed and pushed her away from him. 'No, not crab-apples. But maybe I mistook apples for lemons.'

'Well, I like that!' exclaimed Crysten. Her eyes were fixed on his face and she was laughing, too. She saw the little lines between his eyes and the dark hair curling around his ears. She lifted her hand to touch it.

And then she remembered.

CHAPTER THREE

AFTERWARDS, Crysten was never sure what it was that had brought the memories rippling back. Maybe it was the way Gregg's ear curved against his head, or something about the angle of his nose, but suddenly she knew where she had seen that arresting face before.

She had been a young girl, and her older sister, Joy, had come home laughing and giggling with a group of friends. They were making a great deal of noise, and the cause of all the high spirits was a girl called Sally—who had just announced her engagement. Sally's fiancé was the son of a wealthy local businessman—and his name was Gregg Malleson.

Crysten, hovering on the edge of the crowd, and fascinated by this glimpse of the romance and excitement of grown-up life, had gone shyly up to Sally and asked her if she had a picture of her young man, who for some reason had not accompanied his intended bride that evening.

Sally, intoxicated by all the attention, had hastily pulled a photograph out of her wallet and handed it to Crysten. It was of a much younger, less intense-looking Gregg. The face in the picture was not smiling, but it was a boyish, happy face, filled with enthusiasm for life, and there were none of the lines of experience and disillusion which were so obvious now. She had studied the picture of that younger Gregg for some time, because when she went to give it back, Sally had disappeared. In the end,

Crysten had given it to Joy to return to its owner.

Now, standing so close to the current reality of that face seen long ago in a photograph, Crysten remembered the aftermath of that noisy, exuberant evening.

The wedding date had been set, and Joy had received an invitation, although Sally was not a very close friend. Then, only a week before the marriage was to take place, Joy had come home looking puzzled and disappointed, and announced that Gregg had broken off the engagement. Sally said he had fallen for somebody else and had callously decided to dump her. According to Joy, poor Sally was completely heart-broken and was crying herself to sleep every night. As far as Crysten could remember, she had not heard Sally spoken of again.

As memories of the past faded, and Crysten realised she was still standing in front of Gregg with one hand extended towards his face, she took a hasty step backwards and brushed her hand at her hair instead.

Watching her, Gregg's smile vanished, and she saw small white lines appear beside his mouth.

'Now what's wrong?' His voice was impatient. 'I thought we were getting along quite well for a change.'

'Of course. Why shouldn't we be?' Crysten was smiling very brightly. 'But we mustn't take these things too seriously, must we? After all, a kiss is just a kiss, and there are other fish in the pond besides you.'

She knew she sounded like a twittery little flirt, but she couldn't help herself. This man had the power to hurt her. More than she wanted to admit. And he was quite capable of doing to her what he had done to Sally. She had known Gregg was arrogant and sometimes tyrannical, but now she knew that the thing which had bothered her most about him, the shadow that had drifted at the back of her mind ever since she met him, had been the memory of a happy, laughing girl whose joy had turned to ashes at the hands of an uncaring, selfish male. Yes, he was arrogant. But worse, far worse, he was hard and unfeeling, concerned only with his own pleasure and satisfaction.

Yet looking at him now, seeing the angry confusion in his eyes, she wasn't sure. He had been very young at the time ... No! That way lay only heartache and unhappiness. She was not going to spend *her* nights crying over this desperately attractive man.

But as soon as she made the decision, Gregg, who had been watching her closely, took a step forward and seized both her arms in a hard, painful grip. He loomed over her, looking like some avenging devil from the pages of medieval legend.

'All right, Crysten,' he was saying now, in a cold, tight voice that sent shivers up her spine. 'Have it your own way. While we're on the subject of fish, I am not playing bedtime snack to your barracuda, and there is not the slightest danger of me taking you too seriously. Obviously you have never been serious in your life.'

'You're a fine one to talk!' snapped Crysten, trying to free her arms and finding them pinned against her sides. Her eyes glittered daggers and she could feel the blood surging through her veins.

'Am I?' His voice was like ice cracking on a frozen river.

'Yes, you are!' shouted Crysten, not caring that Sheila and Doris were probably all ears. 'Have you forgotten Sally?'

She saw his dark face turn very white, and his eyes,

which had been deep and angry, were suddenly blank and distant.

'Sally? No, I haven't forgotten Sally. How could I. She's the woman you reminded me of.'

Crysten stopped trying to free her arms and stared at him. Yes, of course! Joy had assured her she would grow up to look just like Sally when, as a girl, she had sighed and wished she could be as pretty as the newly engaged woman. Gregg must like the type, then. But only for as long as it amused him. If she let him get close to her heart, *she* would one day become a 'memory that's better forgotten'.

As the pressure on her arms increased and she began to wonder if he was trying to turn them into pretzels, Crysten felt a force build up inside her which at any moment was going to explode.

'Do you mind?' she spat. 'I would appreciate it if you would let me go. Now! Just because I reminded you that you once jilted a girl, there's no need to behave like a deranged gorilla. I am *not* one of your rolls of linoleum, or even a case of rusty nails.'

Gregg released her arms immediately. As she staggered back, Crysten was amazed to see that his fury had been replaced by something which looked almost like amusement. There was a curious gleam in his eyes as he replied unevenly. 'Not rusty nails, Crysten.' Yes, his shoulders were definitely shaking. 'A crabby apple you may be, but not a rusty nail.'

Crysten's rage began to subside. It was no good, she couldn't stay angry with this man for long. The only thing she *could* do was get away from him as fast as possible and make certain she never saw him again. She wondered at her sense of loss—just as she wondered why her banal remarks about not getting serious should have produced such a blazing reaction. But, in spite of his fury, Gregg seemed to have the ability to reduce high drama to the ridiculous with surprising speed. A crabby apple, indeed! Well, at least that was better than a barracuda.

She gave him a frosty little smile, picked up her bag, and said she had better be leaving.

He nodded. The amused expression had vanished as quickly as it appeared, and his features were smooth and expressionless as he opened the door for her, and thanked her again for solving the mystery of the late delivery.

'You're very welcome. Any time,' said Crysten blandly, as she waved goodbye to Sheila and Doris and started down the stairs.

Now that was a foolish thing to say. She had no intention of coming back here again—not any time, or ever.

But of course it didn't matter, because there was no way Gregg would ask her again—ever.

'Aha! She's calling her boyfriend.' Dan the office boy's cheeky face appeared round the doorway as Crysten picked up the phone. Behind him, Don from the mailroom pulled a face at her.

'You know what she's going to say?' said Dan, his voice an exaggerated whisper. 'She's going to tell him she's crazy about him, that she can't bear to be parted from him even for an hour, that her heart beats like a drum whenever he comes near . . .'

'Does Crysten *have* a boyfriend?' asked Don interestedly.

'I don't know.' Dan waved the question away. 'But anyway, she's telling him he's wonderful, so strong and handsome that she couldn't live without him . . .'

'As a matter of fact,' interrupted Crysten repressively, 'I'm ordering toilet paper.'

Dan's turgid eloquence had to be nipped in the bud if she was to avoid dissolving into helpless giggles the moment she was connected to the Sales Department of Hannigan's Bathroom Supplies. It was virtually impossible to remain serious when he was in a teasing mood—which was almost always.

'She got you that time, Dan,' chortled his friend.

Never one to mind admitting defeat, Dan agreed that she had, and both young men, with cheery waves to Crysten, ambled off down the corridor.

Crysten, who really *was* ordering toilet paper, along with paper towels and soap, finished her conversation with Hannigan's and turned to the letter she was drafting for Mr Jacobsen.

But Dan's joking comments had distracted her. Raine was so happy with her Bill. Maybe it would be nice to have someone who was so wonderful she couldn't live without him . . . Funny, she'd never felt that way before. She had valued her independence too much . . . It had been almost two weeks since that disconcerting meeting with Gregg Malleson . . . Now wait a minute! It certainly wasn't possible that *he* had anything to do with her sudden yearning for romance.

Mr Jacobsen said Gregg had called to thank Getaway for clearing up the matter of the late deliveries, and that particular complaint file had been closed with a satisfactory snap.

Very satisfactory, decided Crysten, determinedly

seizing her pen, and pulling a yellow pad from her drawer.

But Mr Jacobsen's letter seemed fated to remain unwritten. She was just writing the words 'Last time we phoned your Customer Service Department we were informed that it had gone home, so perhaps we can be forgiven for wondering if it is ever at work'—she was sure Mr Jacobsen would veto that line, but it relieved her feelings—when she looked up from her desk to see her employer's head peering round the door.

To her surprise, the expression on his face was almost—she searched for the right word—guilty. Yes, guilty. There was no other way to describe it.

'Good afternoon, Mr Jacobsen,' Crysten greeted him warily, as he strolled in with his hands in his pockets. She had a feeling that whatever he had come to see her about was something he did not expect her to like.

He cleared his throat. An ominous sign. If the news was good he always launched straight into it with no pause or hesitation.

This time the pause was lengthy and was followed by more throat clearing. What *was* he going to say?

'Mr Jacobsen . . .' she began.

'Crysten . . .' They were speaking in unison.

She waited for him to go on.

'Crysten, I have a proposition to put to you.'

She raised her eyebrows. 'Really, Mr Jacobsen?'

'No, no, not that kind of proposition.' The comfortably married man was almost blushing. 'It's just that I've been asked to release you from our employment— temporarily, of course. For a matter of a couple of weeks.' He clasped his hands firmly behind his back, raised himself on his toes and gazed fixedly at a mark high up on the wall.

Crysten was mystified. 'But why?' she asked, her voice bewildered. And then, as another thought occurred to her, '*Who* asked you?'

Mr Jacobsen removed his eyes from the wall and stared at the floor instead. 'Gregg Malleson,' he muttered.

'Did you say . . .?' No, she must have heard wrong. '*Who* did you say asked you?' she repeated.

'Gregg Malleson of Malleson Enterprises. He was so impressed with the work you did for him that he wants you as his personal assistant for a special project of his. It involves some travel, I believe.'

'And of course you said it was impossible,' said Crysten, fixing her employer with her best steely stare, and trying desperately to hide the shock of excitement which had gone through her at the mention of Gregg's name. She was sure it must show on her face.

'Well—er—no. No, I didn't say it was *impossible*,' replied Mr Jacobsen. 'You see, I've owed his father a favour for some time. Glad to repay it. Besides——' a small and hastily concealed twinkle appeared in his eye '—fond of you, my dear. You've been an asset to Getaway. Glad to see you have this opportunity. Gregg's a nice young man.'

Crysten remembered the last occasion on which she had encountered Gregg, and wondered what Mr Jacobsen found so nice about him.

'That,' she stated with conviction, 'has nothing to do with it, Mr Jacobsen. I can't understand why Gregg would ask for me, anyway. I really don't think he likes me much. And I certainly don't like him.'

'Don't you? What a pity. But of course he likes you.

Says you're efficient, well organised and just what he needs.'

Mr Jacobsen's kindly spoken words only increased her confusion. She couldn't for the life of her see why Gregg should have been all that impressed with her efforts. She had only discovered what he could easily have found out for himself if he had taken the trouble to try. Unless—Mr Jacobsen had not actually told her what the project was. Perhaps what Gregg had in mind had nothing to do with business. Two weeks was just about the right length of time for a little extra-curricular activity in Hawaii—or a passionate interlude in the Bahamas.

As soon as the thought crossed her mind she was furious with herself, because in spite of her intention to refuse whatever Gregg suggested, she found her heart was beating very fast and there was a strange burning sensation in her limbs.

Mr Jacobsen scuttled away, muttering that he hoped she would accept. Half an hour later Gregg called her up, expecting to discuss the details of his project—and it was not Hawaii or the Bahamas that he proposed, but Winnipeg, Manitoba.

CHAPTER FOUR

'WINNIPEG!' yelped Crysten, forgetting that she had no intention of going anywhere with him. 'But it could be snowing in Winnipeg at this time of year.'

'So what?' replied Gregg impatiently. 'It rains here.' Then he hesitated. 'Didn't Mark explain to you what I wanted?'

'No, he did not. He just told me you had some project going and wanted my services for two weeks. He didn't say what kind of services.' As soon as the words were out, she was glad Gregg couldn't see her face, which had turned an unattractive shade of puce.

'Oh.' He sounded put out, almost as though, for once, he didn't know what to say.

'In any case,' she said, before he could go any further. 'I'm afraid I won't be available.'

'Don't invent difficulties, Crysten.' Gregg was at his most dictatorial now. 'Of course you'll be available. Mark Jacobsen says there's no problem at all.'

'And I suppose it hasn't occurred to you,' replied Crysten sweetly, 'that I might make plans for my life outside office hours?'

There was silence at the other end of the line. When Gregg finally spoke, Crysten thought that for the second time in the course of this conversation, she detected a faint note of uncertainty.

'No, I suppose it hadn't. But you're right. I should have

considered that possibility. *Have* you made plans that can't be changed?'

'No,' mumbled Crysten in a very small voice.

Damn! Why was it that she couldn't lie to this man? She was an expert liar when it came to explaining to persistent salesmen that Mr Jacobsen was out for the day, when in fact he was down the hall visiting the coffee machine. She had not been too bad at fending off unwanted suitors for Raine, either, in the days before Bill had appeared on the scene. But she couldn't lie to Gregg, who now sounded irritatingly smug as he suggested that, in that case, perhaps she would come over to his house that evening to discuss the matter.

'I'm not going to your house,' snapped Crysten. 'And I'm not discussing the matter any further. It's out of the question.'

'Why? Oh, I see. Don't worry, you'll be adequately chaperoned. My housekeeper will be in tonight. Besides, I told you before, I don't ravish innocent maidens before dinner.'

'What about after dinner?' asked Crysten without thinking.

'Well, anything to oblige, of course . . .'

She heard the laughter in his voice and cursed herself. 'I didn't mean that,' she said quickly, knowing she had meant exactly that. Why couldn't she just hang up the phone and cut this ridiculous conversation off before she got in any deeper?

But she didn't hang up, and a few minutes later she found that somehow she had agreed to visit Gregg that evening to discuss the details of a business trip to Winnipeg.

'Did you tell him you *would* go, then?' asked Raine, as

she watched Crysten slip into a sexy scarlet dress with a low-cut back, and then discard it in favour of a baggy white shirt and jeans.

'No, of course not. I really don't know why I'm seeing him at all.' Crysten had removed the baggy shirt and was substituting a lacy blouse.

'Probably so you can try on your entire wardrobe before Gregg the Great arrives to pick you up,' replied Raine drily.

Crysten paused in the act of unbuttoning the blouse to grin sheepishly at her friend.

'Gregg the Grim, you mean. But you're right. This is crazy, isn't it? What shall I wear?'

'*Not* the red dress, unless you want to incite him to uncontrollable passion on the rug of 2A, Chaffinch Apartments. Which I wouldn't advise. This rug has seen better days as it is, and it doesn't need any finishing touches.'

Crysten giggled. 'The dress isn't *that* bad,' she protested.

'No, it's a very good dress—if rape's what you have in mind.'

'Oh, all right. I'll save it for the right occasion, and settle for dainty lace and my most demure blue skirt.'

Studying Crysten as she finished combing her hair and began to apply lipstick, Raine thought that for someone who swore she wasn't interested in the job anyway, her friend was going to an awful lot of trouble with her appearance. And the blue skirt wasn't making much difference. Sexy red, or demure blue, her room-mate still looked very alluring.

Gregg must have thought so too, because the look he gave her when he knocked on the door, and then opened it without waiting for an answer, was one of unqualified admiration.

'You look almost edible,' he told her, staring appreciatively at the curves of her neat figure.

Then his brows lifted quickly as his eyes fell on the red dress which Crysten had thrown over the sofa. He sauntered across the room and picked it up. Thoughtfully he studied the dress, then glanced appraisingly at Crysten. His eyebrows were still raised and there was a small, intimate smile on his lips as he remarked approvingly, 'Very promising, Star. What made you decide against it?'

Crysten felt herself turning the same colour as the dress.

'I didn't decide against it.' She refused to look at him. 'I was just seeing if it needed cleaning.'

'Ah, I see.' He tried to make her meet his eyes, but gave up when she wouldn't look at him and appeared totally absorbed by a lurid poster of a rock group which Bill had once given to Raine. Gregg studied the ceiling instead. Crysten, snatching a surreptitious glance at his face, saw a faint smile flick the edge of his mouth.

'We'd better go,' she muttered, hastily introducing him to Raine as she hurried towards the door.

But, as Gregg opened it for her, Raine pulled her back and whispered, 'Wow! If I didn't already have Bill, I'd be sorely tempted. Didn't know they made them like that any more.'

'They don't,' muttered Crysten. 'Packaging can be deceiving.'

But as she watched him run down the stairs to unlock the Rover, she had to admit that the package ahead of her in the casual white shirt and hip-hugging beige trousers was really quite breathtakingly attractive.

'OK, so what's this job all about?' she asked, as the car sped out of town towards the mountains.

'Patience, Miss Starr. All will be revealed. Over the excellent meal that Mrs Bedford is preparing for us—at least, I hope she is.'

'Who's Mrs Bedford?' Crysten was annoyed that he had mistaken her natural curiosity for impatience about his proposition—which she was going to turn down anyway.

'Mrs B is my housekeeper, cook, support in every conceivable crisis and part-time mother of my son. Without her, my life would be an impossible series of disasters.'

Hearing the genuine warmth in his voice, Crysten wondered what had happened to Mr Bedford, and whether this paragon was destined to become the future Mrs Malleson. She was also surprised to hear Gregg admit so readily to dependence on his housekeeper. She had thought of him as totally self-sufficient, and removed from the minor irritations that plagued people like herself. But that was foolish. Of course he was human. Very much so.

He gave her a slow, sensual smile which made her breath catch in her throat. Without reservation now, she smiled back. Suddenly he was not the ogre she had imagined, but a very sexy, fascinating man—and Sally was a long time ago.

He took one large hand from the wheel and placed it over hers.

'Don't worry, Crysten. Mrs B will look after you.'

'I wasn't worrying,' she muttered—but when he took his hand away, she felt a sharp jab of disappointment.

Gregg's house was a large, rambling edifice of wood and white stucco, which looked as though bits had been added on year by year at the whims of owners with widely differing tastes. It was set on a hillside in West Vancouver and, through the trees which surrounded the big, shaded garden, Crysten caught a glimpse of the waters of the Inlet. The lights of a small boat drifted by and then were lost to view.

'Oh, it's lovely!' she cried. 'Everything looks as though it's been here for ever.'

'Well, since the beginning of the century, anyway,' he replied, helping her out of the car. 'I grew up here. When my mother died, Loni and I moved back with Dad. My son was born here.' There was something strained in the way he spoke now, and Crysten was puzzled.

'Was Loni your wife? She didn't have your son in the hospital, then?'

'No. We didn't get there in time. She died when Jimmy was born.' There was no mistaking the bleakness in his voice now, and Crysten wished she had not asked.

'I'm sorry. I didn't mean . . .'

'It's all right.' The harsh lines of his face faded and he smiled at her. 'I was the one who brought it up. Come on.'

He seized her hand and towed her behind him into the house. For a moment she felt like a leaf in the wake of a hurricane. Didn't Gregg ever move at a normal pace?

All she noticed as he whisked her through the hallway was the unusually high ceiling and a carved oak chest supporting a collection of shining copper kettles. Then they were in a large, bright room with windows overlooking the darkened garden. In an alcove in the corner a small table was set for two. Big soft couches lined three walls and on the fourth was an old oak bookcase. Most of the books seemed to be about building and home repairs, but Crysten was amused to see that there was also a large dictionary prominently on display.

'This is my favourite room,' Gregg told her as he led her to a seat near the window.

While he went to fetch drinks Crysten was left to look about her. Her overall impression was of comfort, beautifully carved oak and a lot more highly polished copper. So perhaps Gregg did occasionally find time to unwind and enjoy the pleasures of a warm, relaxing evening.

In a moment he returned carrying two glasses of pale, sparkling liquid.

'Champagne?' she asked, taking the glass and turning to smile at him.

'Of course. To celebrate our partnership.' He lowered his long body down beside her and stretched an arm along the back of the couch. She felt his fingers run casually through the curls at the back of her neck and deep inside her something twisted alarmingly. She turned startled eyes on his face. The fingers dropped easily over her shoulder as he leant against the arm of the couch and studied her openly, his dark eyes unusually wide and intent.

'What partnership? And what are you looking at?' she asked, uncomfortably conscious of his nearness, yet unable, or unwilling, to move away.

'You. Did you know there were freckles on your nose? They suit you.'

Crysten was well aware of the freckles and didn't think they suited her at all. She took a quick sip from her glass and sneezed.

'Bubbles go up your nose?' he asked sympathetically,

handing her a clean white handkerchief.

She nodded. 'Mm. They always do. I love champagne, but it usually makes me sneeze.'

He laughed, a deep infectious laugh that sent odd, exciting sensations down her spine. She started to laugh too, with a careless, surprising abandon.

When Mrs Bedford came in, carrying a linen-covered tray laden with mysterious dishes, she found the two of them still laughing. Gregg was holding a handkerchief to Crysten's nose and trying to persuade her to blow.

'Now, now,' admonished Mrs Bedford. 'You young people settle down and eat your dinners. Time enough for fun and games later.'

'Yes, Mrs B,' said Gregg meekly. 'Whatever you say.' There was a wicked gleam in his eyes that caused Mrs Bedford to remark tartly that *that* would be the day, when he ever did what he was told.

Crysten smiled at the portly, grey-haired woman and told her she could well believe that Gregg was a law unto himself.

'Well, you're right enough there,' agreed Mrs Bedford emphatically, laying the tray on the table and starting to uncover dishes. 'Come along now. Sit down and eat.'

Gregg sighed and made a face. 'I'm fated to spend my life in the clutches of bossy women,' he complained. 'I have to put up with Sheila at work and when I come home, looking for a bit of peace and quiet, what do I find . . .?'

'Food,' said Mrs Bedford implacably. 'Sit. Both of you.'

They sat.

Crysten remembered the tyrant she had seen ruling the roost at the Malleson Enterprises, and smiled.

'She's a dear—and a match even for you,' she chuckled, when Mrs Bedford had left them dutifully consuming roast chicken. 'Wherever did you find her?'

'She's more than a match for me, I assure you,' replied Gregg gloomily. But the eyes which met hers over a forkful of chicken were filled with amused affection. 'She's been with us for eight years now. Ever since Loni died. She lost her husband years ago and has no one of her own left—so we've taken the place of family for her.'

'You're lucky.' Crysten took a sip from the glass of wine which Gregg had poured. 'When you first mentioned her, I thought maybe she was the next Mrs Malleson.'

'God forbid!' Gregg rolled his eyes at the ceiling.

They finished the chicken, followed by a rich creamy cake which drove Crysten to frantic mental surveys of the local diet and exercise clubs. Then Gregg suggested she might like to walk in the garden.

'To work off that wonderful dinner?' she asked, jumping to her feet with alacrity.

'Yes, if you like.' He smiled. 'But I also need to talk to you—so don't get too involved with the weight loss programme. You look just fine as you are.' He held out his hand. 'Come on.'

Crysten hesitated. How had he known she worried about her weight? She glanced at his face, and seeing the mocking gleam in his eyes knew that he had also guessed she was afraid to touch him. She drew a quick breath and placed her hand in his.

Funny how right it felt to be wandering hand in hand in the October darkness with this autocratic giant who for once in his life was moving at a normal speed. But even now she sensed that she was walking beside a core of suppressed energy that might erupt at any moment.

To her relief the volcano remained dormant, and after they had passed through a maze of dim, bush-lined paths they came to a path of dark green grass on a slope overlooking the water. He pulled her down beside him.

It was cold and the grass was damp. Crysten shivered. After a while he put his arm round her. She held her breath. But when she looked at the dark profile silhouetted against the fading lights of the bay, she saw that he was staring across the water with an expression so strange and distant that she was afraid to open her mouth.

At last she heard him exhale quietly and, when he turned his head, his voice was cool and devoid of emotion.

'You're remarkably like her,' he said.

'Like who?'

'Sally.'

She tried to shift away from him, but his arm still held her body against his shoulder.

'Yes, of course. Sally,' she repeated, in a voice as cool as his.

Abruptly he released her, and again she was surprised and disturbed by the sensation that she had lost something precious.

'Never mind,' he continued. 'With luck, you're nothing like her on the inside. Shall we get down to business?'

'If you like.' Crysten replied warily. She pulled at a blade of grass. It broke. What was the matter with this man? One minute he was full of fun and laughter and the next he was all power and business—and Sally. Yes, she must remember Sally—who had been so badly hurt by the man sitting beside her now.

As she wrenched her mind away from the past, she realised he was explaining about the trip to Winnipeg, and that he wanted her to go with him.

'Why Winnipeg? And why me?' She was warier than ever.

'Because I'm in the process of buying out a business there. Johnson Exteriors. Negotiations start next week and I don't trust Uriah Johnson. I want the entire meeting recorded in detail, so he can't try to backtrack later. As for "why you?"—well, Mark Jacobsen tells me you take shorthand.'

'Yes, I do. But why don't you just tape the meeting?'

'Because old Uriah won't negotiate with machines in the room. At least, that's what he says. But he can't argue if I bring my assistant.

'Sheila's your assistant. Why don't you take her?'

'Sheila's my secretary and I need her to run the place while I'm away. Besides, she doesn't take shorthand. OK? Objections overruled?'

Crysten saw his body move restlessly in the darkness and resisted an urge to reach out and touch him, to run her fingers through the thick, dark hair ...

Stop it, she told herself firmly. I must remember Sally.

'Yes, objections overruled,' she agreed quickly. 'But of course I can't go.'

'Of course you *can*.' Gregg's voice was a forceful blast in the silence of the night. 'Don't be a mule, Crysten.'

'I'm not a mule!' she cried, jumping to her feet and accidentally kicking his thigh. 'And I'm not sitting out here turning into an icicle just so you can call me names.'

'Ouch!' replied Gregg, uncoiling his length from the ground and moving to stand over her. 'I believe you're right. You've got hooves like the devil's apprentice. No mule could compete.' He ran his hand cautiously down his bruised thigh and Crysten's eyes were drawn to the outline of his legs. They seemed even longer as he stood, legs apart, in the moonlight like some ancient god of darkness.

'I am not the devil's apprentice either,' she spat, turning quickly away and starting to run towards the house. But he caught up with her before she had gone three yards, and she felt his hand grip her shoulder as he swung her round to face him.

'Don't fight with me, Star,' he said softly, as his thumb stroked up and down her neck. 'All I want is a business arrangement for two weeks. Nothing else, I promise.'

He bent his head and she thought she felt his lips brush very gently across her forehead. 'Will you come, Crysten?'

She shivered, and wondered what that brief caress had had to do with a business arrangement.

'Maybe. Can we talk about this in the light—where I can see your face?'

'Do you want to see it? That's a beginning, anyway.' Crysten heard the laughter in his voice and there was a sinking feeling in her stomach, because she had a sudden intuition that she was going to lose this battle of wills to the overpowering man beside her.

'All right,' she said a few minutes later when they were seated at a discreet distance from each other across the table. 'Have I got this straight? You want me to fly to Winnipeg with you, take notes of your meetings with Uriah Johnson—and the rest of my time is my own?'

Gregg ran a hand carelessly through his hair. 'More or less,' he agreed. 'Only we're not flying. My father is coming, too. He thinks he needs new glasses.'

'He's going to Winnipeg for new glasses?'

Gregg smiled. 'Believe it or not, yes. All his life he's seen Dr Boyko about his eyes, and now the old fellow has retired to Winnipeg. He has a daughter there. Dad refuses to see anyone else, so I'm taking him along with me. On the train, because his doctor here advises him not to fly.' He grinned. 'Besides, I've always been fascinated by trains.'

'Mm,' murmured Crysten. 'All that power and noise. It fits your personality.'

'Is that what you think of me? Power and noise?'

'Only partly,' she admitted, watching the sensual curve of his lips.

He shrugged and his eyes went blank. 'It doesn't matter, anyway. This is strictly a business proposition—since you've told me you're not interested in anything more—stimulating. However, you can solve a problem for me, and I can pay you well and offer you a free holiday into the bargain. Do you accept?'

There was a challenge in his voice. Crysten had always found it hard to resist a dare, and she was very sure that being close to Gregg for two weeks and keeping strictly, or even mostly, to business, would be more than just a challenge. But . . .

She thought of the little Honda she had just bought which was eating so much of her salary. She could certainly use the extra money.

Gregg saw the indecision in her eyes and pressed his advantage. 'I'll double what Jacobsen's paying you.'

Afterwards she could never decide whether it was the money that had made up her mind for her, or the compelling magnetism of his eyes. But whichever it was, there was no doubt at all that the voice saying, 'Yes, all right. I'll come,' was her own, even if it did come out like a mouse whose squeak needed oiling.

'Raine, do you think I'm out of my mind?' Crysten asked her friend, when she returned home later that evening in a state of confusion which she was certain must border on the unbalanced.

Raine regarded her thoughtfully, her brown eyes unusually serious.

'I don't know. Not if you like this man enough to risk getting hurt. He's the type who could hurt a woman very easily, I think. I doubt if he'd even know he was doing it.'

'Why do you say that?'

'Because he's devastatingly attractive, and from the little I've seen of him, I'd say he's not particularly aware of it. But I think he's used to getting what he wants when he wants it.' She grinned. 'He's got you going to Winnipeg with him anyway, and you swore that was the last thing you'd do.'

Crysten ran a finger along the back of a chair and stared absently at the floor. 'I know. I can't understand it myself. He's very persuasive, of course . . .'

'Obviously. Crysten, don't be a goose. I've lived with you for three years and I've never seen you anything but cheerful, sure of yourself and happily uninvolved with the men you date. Lately you've been dreamy, moody and totally befuddled. Don't you know you're falling in love with that handsome hulk of virility?'

The expression on Raine's face was almost fierce, and Crysten saw that her friend was genuinely worried about her.

'Of course I'm not falling in love!' she scoffed. 'Gregg *is* very attractive—and when he stops ordering people around he can be amusing and fun to be with. But I'm certainly not in love with him. I can use the money and a holiday, that's all.'

But deep down, she wondered if Raine could be right. Apart from passionate schoolgirl infatuations, she had never been seriously in love. Would she even know what if felt like?

Raine had turned away and was busily straightening cushions. 'Did you meet his father?' she asked, changing the subject.

'No. He was playing bridge with friends. Gregg says he's a bit of a night-hawk. I didn't meet his son, either. I think he was staying overnight somewhere—with one of the kids in his class. Anyway, I'll meet Malleson senior on Monday when we leave for Winnipeg.'

'Yes, so you will.' Raine's voice was determinedly non-committal.

Crysten resisted an urge to shout at her friend to stop being such a damned know-it-all, and with an abrupt 'goodnight', she stumbled off to bed, making a firm resolve that under no circumstances was she going to dream about Gregg Malleson.

She didn't. Instead she fell into a deep, warm sleep from which she awoke in the morning full of excitement and optimism. Raine was wrong. She was not in the least in love with Gregg and she was going to have a wonderful time on the train, which she had never travelled on before. Winnipeg was new to her too, and, snow or no snow, she was going to enjoy it.

But on the afternoon when she hurried out of the rain and into the protective shelter of the old Canadian National Station, she was not so sure. At first there was

no sign of Gregg, and when she did find him he was
standing at the ticket counter with a face like a
thunderstorm, shouting at a small boy who was scuttling
away from a pile of luggage. 'Get the hell back where I
told you,' he bawled, 'and don't you move one inch away
from that baggage!'

The child's mouth turned down sulkily, but he
returned to the luggage, sat down on a large brown
suitcase and started to play with the lock.

'And leave that lock alone, too!' yelled Gregg.

Crysten's eyes turned from the irate man at the counter
to the child whose lower lip was now stuck out at an
obstinate angle which would have left her in no doubt
about his parentage, even if the dark curls and deep-set
eyes had not given it away.

She hesitated, and then walked up behind Gregg. 'I'm
here,' she announced cautiously.

He swung round. 'About time! I told you you should let
me pick you up.'

'I'm in plenty of time and there was no need,' replied
Crysten calmly. 'Have you got my ticket?'

'Of course I've got your ticket. I'm not totally
incompetent.'

'No, just bad-tempered.'

'You'd be bad-tempered too, if you'd suddenly been
landed with a juvenile delinquent who thinks lighted
fireworks are for Show and Tell.'

The ticket agent coughed and the conversation was cut
short.

'Could you persuade my son to get his hands out of my
briefcase?' requested Gregg over his shoulder. Hearing
the note of desperation in his voice, Crysten hoisted her
shoulder-bag and walked over to the boy.

'Hi,' she said. 'I'm Crysten. You must be Jimmy.'

'Yes,' he replied, obligingly removing sticky fingers from a bound leather folder inside the briefcase. 'I am. But I think my Dad wishes I wasn't.'

'I'm sure he doesn't wish any such thing. I know he's very proud of you. He told me you want to be a hockey player when you grow up.'

'Well, I did.' He kicked glumly at the side of a suitcase. 'But Dad says there's no chance of that now. He says the National Hockey League doesn't take pyro—pyro . . .' He hesitated, stumbling over the word, then finally got it out. 'He says they don't take pyromaniacs.'

CHAPTER FIVE

'THEY don't take *what*?' gasped Crysten. 'Whatever do you mean, Jimmy?'

Jimmy's lower lip protruded even further as he stole a doubtful look at his father.

'Well, I had this rocket, you see. My friend gave it me. It was s'posed to be for Hallowe'en, only I thought it would be neat to take it to school. I'm in Grade Three,' he added proudly.

'Good for you. But you don't mean you actually lit it?'

'Uh-huh. Mike and I did. It was Show and Tell. We thought it would just go off and make everyone jump.'

'And did it?'

'Oh, yes! It made a great bang.' For a moment his sullen expression changed and the small face lit up at the memory of past noise. Then dejection returned and he added sadly. 'But we didn't know it would hit the ceiling and bounce off Mrs Mikelchuk's desk on to Cassandra Zinger's model theatre and land in the baseball cap John Sawyer had stolen off Arnie McLaughlin.'

Crysten, listening open-mouthed to this tale of multiple disaster, tried desperately to control the quiver in her voice.

'Oh, dear. Was there very much damage?'

'Well, sort of. Arnie McLaughlin tried to save his cap and John Sawyer wouldn't let him and he threw it at the window. But he missed and the curtains caught fire. So did Cassandra's theatre. I don't think she's speaking to me any more.' He gave a long, lugubrious sigh.

'Oh, dear,' repeated Crysten faintly. 'What did Mrs Mikelchuk do?'

'She was great. She tore the curtains down and stuffed them in the dustbin. Then she turned it upside down over Cassandra's theatre and Arnie's cap.'

'That was quick thinking. How lucky for everyone that she knew what to do.' Now Crysten was sure she was going to choke.

'It wasn't lucky for Mrs Mikelchuk. Her hands got burnt and she had to have big wet bandages on them.'

'Poor Mrs Mikelchuk.'

'Mm, and she was real nice about it, too. She said she knew we didn't mean to start a fire. We didn't either. I like school. But they had to close our classroom because of smoke damage or something and Mr Rejo—he's the Principal—he said Mike and me had better stay home for a week. So now I have to go to Winnipeg with Dad because Mrs Bedford has the 'flu.'

'I see. You don't sound very pleased. Don't you like trains?'

'Oh, sure. But Dad doesn't like me. He says I'm a pyro—pyromaniac—and a bloody nuisance, and a little son of a . . .'

'Jimmy!' roared a voice from behind them. 'That is quite enough.'

Crysten turned quickly. Gregg's face looked more thunderous than ever, and now that she could see it properly she noticed that there was a deep cut running down one cheek which had not been there the last time she had seen him.

'Goodness, what did you do to yourself?' she asked.

'I played hockey last night. Got hit by a stick,' he replied curtly.

'Yes, he's got three stitches,' Jimmy chipped in. 'I don't think Dad's very good at hockey. Last time he played he got a black eye. It was neat.'

'Jimmy, I told you to shut up,' growled Gregg.

'I know, but . . .'

'No buts. Let's get moving. Where's your case, Crysten?'

She indicated the holdall, and he raised his eyebrows. 'That's it?'

'Yes. I always travel light.'

'Hm. You're the first woman I've ever travelled with who did.'

Was that a grudging kind of admiration she heard in his voice? She wasn't given time to ponder over it because the next moment he had grabbed Jimmy and a suitcase in one hand, hoisted the remainder of the luggage over his shoulder and was striding rapidly across the hard, polished floor towards the platform. Crysten regretted her fancy red shoes and wished she had remembered that, with a man like Gregg around, runners were the only kind of footwear that made any sense. Just the same, for the moment she was almost sorry for the boss of Malleson Enterprises. To start off a business trip with a face that made him look like the survivor of a street fight was bad enough. But to be lumbered with an enterprising eight-year-old who had just been suspended for arson must have been the last straw. No wonder Gregg's well-publicised charm was not much in evidence today.

He was way ahead of her now, pounding down the platform past the dome-car, then past two blue and yellow carriages and the silver dining-car. At the fifth carriage he stopped. Crysten saw him turn, and grimace impatiently when he realised she was not right behind him.

'Sorry, you're too fast for me,' she gasped when she caught up. Looking into his glowering dark eyes, she hoped he was not aware that her breathlessness was not entirely caused by running in high heels.

He ignored the apology and jerked his head at the door of the train. 'Get in. You're in Roomette Twelve.'

The blue-coated porter standing by the step pursed his mouth disapprovingly at Gregg's peremptory tone, and a surge of angry humiliation scorched Crysten's cheeks.

'I believe you hired me as your assistant, not your slave,' she said hotly. 'I can't help it if I don't walk at your speed, and it wouldn't hurt you to say please.'

From the corner of her eye she saw the porter nod agreement, and Jimmy's eyes widen in startled admiration. In front of her, Gregg's face turned a livid brick colour. He swallowed, shifted the suitcases on his shoulder, made a sound that was a cross between a laugh and a bark, and admitted that she was quite right, but would she *please* mind getting in because the luggage was wearing out his shoulder and it would be nice to be on board before the train left the station.

Somehow he had managed to put her at a disadvantage again. She gave him her best dignified smile and scrambled up the steps. The porter made an ineffectual grab at the baggage as Gregg climbed up behind her.

'There you are. Roomette Twelve. I hope everything's all right.' His tone was almost conciliatory now.

Crysten saw the hockey injury throbbing on his cheek and remembered the pyromaniac. No, it had not been a good day for Gregg. Under the circumstances, he was entitled to some degree of bad temper.

She decided to forgive and forget. 'It's fine,' she assured him, pulling aside the heavy brown curtain in front of the little cubicle with the red padded seat, round chrome wash-basin and covered toilet.

Her oasis of privacy for the next two days.

'Good. I'll leave you to settle in, then.' He sounded tired. 'I'll see to Jimmy, and we'll meet at dinner.'

'Right.' She had started to unzip her bag when a thought occurred to her. She stuck her head through the curtains and called after him. 'What about your father? I thought he was coming with us.'

Gregg dropped a suitcase on the floor and turned. 'He is. He's already on board. I had to view the damage and pick up Jimmy from school after the pyrotechnics this morning. Dad came on ahead.' He placed a heavy hand on Jimmy's shoulder as the boy started to sidle down the corridor. 'He said the firebug here was *my* son and he had no intention of involving himself in an altercation with the authorities.'

'Was there an altercation?'

'No. Right was entirely on their side.' His eyes met hers and for the first time, Crysten detected a hint that he was beginning to appreciate the humour of the situation. But he still sounded tired.

She placed her toothbrush and toiletries carefully on the wash-basin, kicked off the offending shoes and substituted sandals, then sat down on the seat.

Poor Gregg. He'd certainly had quite a day. And his father, that once energetic founder of Mallesons, was obviously no help. But then, why should he be? Jimmy was all too obviously Gregg's son. She leant her head back on the headrest and wondered what Jimmy's father had been like at school. Just like Jimmy, unless she was vastly mistaken. And Jimmy was only eight. Gregg had quite a few years ahead of him before he could expect much relief from the sort of episode the boy had instigated this morning. It was too bad Loni had died. Undoubtedly Gregg did his best, but he had a business to run—and all those glamorous women to entertain.

Crysten frowned and stared out of the window. The train was starting to move. He would have to do without the glamour for the next few days. Unless—she thought of the sexy red dress she had packed at the bottom of her holdall when she'd hoped Raine wasn't looking. Then she shook her head. She must have been mad. This trip was strictly business. Gregg had made that quite clear.

She closed her eyes on the scrub and gunge that formed the gateway to all city stations, and when she opened them again it was almost dark. Someone was knocking on the door to her roomette.

'Dinner in fifteen minutes,' shouted Gregg. 'I made a reservation for you. We'll collect you on our way to the dining-car.'

She stood up and made a hasty inspection in the mirror. There was a smudge of dirt on her cheek. She ran water into the basin and wiped a cloth over her face. That was better. Now a little blue eyeshadow over the wide grey eyes, a dab of powder on the nose and cheeks, a comb through her blonde hair, and she looked quite presentable. She glanced down at the red slacks and neat black sweater, and had just decided to change them when there was a loud pounding on her door and Gregg's and Jimmy's voices could be heard calling in unison, 'Hurry up. We're on our way to eat.'

Hurry up, indeed! As though there was ever a chance to do anything else if the Malleson family had anything to do with it. She wondered if Gregg's father was the same.

He was. When she edged through the door into the corridor, still wearing her slacks and sweater, she saw a white-haired figure bustling ahead of them around the corner.

'That's Grandpa,' Jimmy informed her. 'He says there's no point waiting around for women, so he's gone on to get a table.'

'I like *that*,' exclaimed Crysten, bristling. 'I'm never late.'

'Nonsense! You were late the first time I saw you— charging into the courthouse like a distraught chicken looking for its head, and almost collapsing with relief when you found you'd made it in time.'

Gregg's eyes mocked her in the semi-darkness of the corridor and she had just opened her mouth to explain to him in concise detail that she did not in the least resemble a headless chicken, and that being almost late was by no means the same as being late, when the train hurtled crazily around a curve and she was knocked off her feet, bounced against the wall and finally ended up slammed against Gregg's chest.

Immediately his arms went up to steady her, and she found herself held fast against his body, looking into black eyes that were regarding her with amusement— and something else. She discovered that she had quite forgotten the lecture she meant to give him. Besides, hadn't he said that he had seen her arriving at the courthouse? That meant he must have been watching her long before she'd noticed him.

His arms were still around her. She felt safe and warm, and the blood was beginning to stir alarmingly in her veins. Gregg was still smiling into her eyes.

'Come on, you two. I'm hungry.' A disgusted voice from behind them brought her back to reality. 'Dad, the train's not rocking any more. Crysten doesn't need holding up. Come on.'

'Doesn't she?' he asked. His eyes met hers in suggestive enquiry as he released her slowly and pushed her ahead of him behind Jimmy, who was rocketing down the corridor like a puppy in pursuit of a ball. His hand was still on her shoulder when they entered the dining-car.

'Hm. At last,' grunted the white-haired man she had seen earlier. From the front he looked like a cross between a bulldog and Spencer Tracy with glasses. He was sitting at a table covered by a white linen cloth, strumming impatiently on a side-plate.

'Miss Starr was ready as soon as I called her,' Gregg placated him. 'Crysten, this is my father, Jake Malleson, without whose inspiration Mallesons would be no more than a neighbourhood hardware store.'

'Humph!' Jake Malleson shot him a suspicious look from under bushy white eyebrows. 'And now I suppose I'm expected to point out that it's your damned blarney and charm that has made Mallesons what it is today. Well, I'm not going to.'

'Good.' Gregg grinned affectionately at his father as the steward pulled out a chair for Crysten. 'Besides, Mallesons hasn't reached its potential by a long way. There'll be plenty of opportunities for Jimmy when he takes over.'

'Huh.' Jake glanced balefully at his grandson. 'Oppor-

tunities for bonfires, you mean. He'll burn the whole lot
down.'

'No, I won't Grandpa. Really. I didn't much like it
when the curtains caught fire. And Cassandra Zinger
won't ever speak to me again. She said so.' He looked so
woebegone that Cyrsten had to smile and assure him
quickly that people often said things they didn't mean
when they were upset, and that she was sure Cassandra
would forgive him.

'She'll probably be missing you by the time you go
back to school,' she finished bracingly.

'D'you think so?' Jimmy brightened. 'Well . . . yes,
maybe she will.'

'Of course she will,' nodded Crysten, starting on her
soup and noticing that Jake Malleson was eyeing her
thoughtfully across the table.

'You're as full of blarney as my son,' he told her. But
she could see the gleam of amused approval in his eye.
Obviously Jake Malleson was exceedingly fond of his
grandson, whatever he might say about bonfires. He
didn't really want the boy to spend the week pining over
Cassandra. Not that Jimmy was likely to spend much
time pining over anything, in Crysten's opinion. He was
too like his father and grandfather who, faced with a
setback in love, would probably throw themselves
forcefully into work—or play. Had Gregg ever had a
setback in love? she mused. He had lost his wife, of
course—and his response to that had certainly not been
to withdraw into a stoical, celibate shell. Not if the social
pages of the paper were anything to go by.

Her reverie was interrupted when she heard Gregg
telling Jimmy that it was time he gave an explanation for
his disgraceful behaviour at school that morning.

Once again Crysten listened to the saga of the vagabond rocket, and as she glanced at Gregg's face she could see the stitches in his cheek tighten.

'I see,' he said, when Jimmy's story was finished. His voice shook slightly as he asked his son what he thought he should do to make amends for the trouble he had caused.

'Well, I already told Mrs Mikelchuk I was sorry,' said Jimmy worriedly. 'Perhaps I could bring her a present. She says she likes chocolates.'

'Yes, that's a good idea,' Gregg agreed. 'But what about the classroom? Someone has to pay for that, you know.'

'Oh.' Jimmy sighed. Then his eyes lit up. 'I know. Mike and me can give Mr Rejo all our savings. Will that be OK? I wanted to buy a racing set. But I guess I'll have to wait.' His shoulders drooped slightly and he glanced pleadingly at his father.

'I guess you will,' replied Gregg implacably, ignoring the plea.

Afterwards, when they had consumed soup, grilled salmon and a doubtful orange tapioca pudding, Jake said he and Jimmy were off to play cards in the club-car.

Some time later Gregg knocked on Crysten's door and asked her if she was asleep.

She put down her book and poked her head out. 'If I had been, I wouldn't be any more, would I?'

He grinned. 'I guess not. What are you doing?'

'Reading, if you must know.'

'No must about it. Just friendly curiosity. Don't be so prickly.'

'Sorry. I didn't mean to be.' She hadn't, either. It was just that whenever Gregg came near her she felt an immediate physical tension which only seemed to find release in snapping his head off. But she hoped he wouldn't go away.

He didn't. Instead he glanced at the title of her book, grinned, and asked if she was reading more steam and sleaze.

'I'm afraid so.' She sighed. 'I haven't had much luck with the books I've picked lately. I think if I read that piece of deathless prose, "her body arched towards him", just one more time, I shall definitely scream.'

Gregg made an odd choking sound which was quickly stifled. 'Then I'll have to come to your rescue,' he replied with a wolfish grin. 'Better make sure you scream loudly.'

'I will.'

'Good. Listen, are you doing anything at the moment?'

'I told you . . .' She saw his dark face in the mirror over the basin and changed her mind. 'No, not really. What is it?'

'I need to talk to someone. Come on up to the dome with me? It's about Jimmy, and it's no use trying my father. He just says he went through it with me and at last he's getting his own back.'

She laughed. 'I bet he did go through it, too. And I don't blame him if he thinks Jimmy serves you right. But I don't see what help I can be.'

'You can listen to me grumble, and hold my hand in the dark and tell me I'm a great father who's doing a wonderful job with that monster who's sleeping in my upper bunk.'

'All right. I'll listen to you grumble if you like, but I'm not telling you you're wonderful. You're convinced enough of that already. And I'm not holding your hand in the dark, either.'

'You're a hard-hearted woman, Crysten Starr. Never mind, it's a deal. Whatever you say.'

But when she was seated beside him in the unlighted dome, watching the dark outlines of trees flash by the curved windows, she found that her hand slipped quite naturally into his. He held it lightly against his knee and gently stroked her fingers.

It was late, and there were no other people sitting above the club-car in the strange, dim quiet which was broken only by the heaving and shunting of the train as it sped purposefully along the track.

Still Gregg continued to stroke her fingers and say nothing. He seemed lost in some brooding reverie in which she had no part. When the silence began to make her uncomfortable, she broke it.

'Why did you want to talk to me about Jimmy?'

His hand tightened around her knuckles. 'Because I worry about him. He should have a mother. I know that, but ...' He shrugged and turned his head away. 'I've been married once. Loni would have been a good mother.'

He relapsed into silence again and Crysten was left wondering what he meant. The words were enigmatic. Had his marriage not been a happy one, then? According to her calculations, it had taken place not long after he had left Sally. Was he incapable of sustaining a long-term relationship, then? Perhaps he was the kind of man who found that once he had what he wanted, he didn't want it any more. If that was the case, Jimmy might be better off without a mother.

But the thought left her feeling cold and deflated. Was Raine right? Was she beginning to fall in love with this forceful, difficult man who had kissed her twice, and both times made the earth stand still and the moon and the stars burst into flames of gold?

When she looked at him again, he seemed to have slouched lower in the seat and his head was very close to hers.

'Gregg . . .?'

He started. 'Sorry. I was dreaming. No, reliving a nightmare would be more accurate.'

'So you do have dreams. Even if they are bad ones.'

'Doesn't everyone?'

'Yes, I suppose they do. But you move so fast I didn't think you had time to dream.'

'Sometimes I haven't.' He touched the scar on his cheek. 'But right now I'm dreaming of Jimmy's future—which doesn't look any too hopeful, does it?'

'Jimmy will be all right. He's just a bright, energetic little boy who doesn't always think before he acts. He's probably a handful for Mrs Bedford, too.'

'He is. As she often says, she's not as young as she used to be. But she's devoted to him.'

'I'm sure she is.' Crysten plucked uneasily at a loose thread in the arm of her seat. 'Perhaps you should spend more time with him yourself.'

He crossed one long leg restlessly over the other. 'How do you know I don't?'

'I can read,' she replied drily.

'Huh. And you believe everything you read, do you? All the silly gossip . . .'

'No, but I doubt if the local paper has a huge stake in printing phoney stories about one of its leading advertisers.'

He gave a reluctant laugh which came out more like a snort. 'OK,' he conceded. 'You win. It's true I'm out a lot.

Business and—other things.' He turned towards her and she felt his thigh brush across her leg. He released her hand and put an arm around her shoulders.

'You like children, don't you?' he asked, as the train shunted suddenly and threw his head against her hair. For a fleeting moment they stayed like that. Then Gregg withdrew his arms and moved away from her.

'I made you a promise, Star,' he murmured. 'Don't let me break it. God knows, I want to.'

She wanted to tell him he could break it any time he liked, especially now, and for a crazy second she longed to put her arms around his neck and run reckless fingers through the waves of his hair—and on, down his back . . .

But before she could stir he had shifted further along the seat, and she could see his hands slapping restlessly on his knee.

Yes, he was attracted to her, there was no doubt about that. But he was the one who had pulled away. Obviously he did not want any involvement. If she wanted to save herself a pile of grief she must fight whatever it was she felt for this man. She was committed to the job on hand, but once it was over she must never see him again. She had said that once before, of course. This time she would make it true.

He was still strumming on his knee. Once more the quietness made her uncomfortable.

'Yes, I do like children,' she said, breaking it with forced vivacity and returning to his earlier question. 'I used to babysit a lot. I enjoyed the kids, provided they stayed dry and quiet.'

Gregg stopped strumming and turned to stare at her. 'You mean that ever happens?' he asked, his lips twitching. 'When Jimmy was born, I think it was a good two years before I could pick him up without the floods beginning. And as for quiet—well, it hasn't happened yet.'

Crysten laughed and relaxed. 'It will,' she assured him.

The train bumped, grunted and lurched to a stop. Gregg rose to his feet.

'We might as well make our way back while it's standing still,' he suggested. 'Ready?'

She stood up, too. 'Any time you are. I'm afraid I haven't been much help about Jimmy.'

'Sure you have.' He grabbed her hand and pulled her down the stairs behind him. 'You've convinced me there's at least a chance he won't grow up to be a master crook.'

'He says he wants to be a hockey player,' replied Crysten reflectively. 'But I expect he'll be a mad tycoon, just like his father.'

They had reached the door of her roomette. Gregg spun her round to face him. 'Mad tycoon, my eye!' he scoffed. 'Hard-working, under-appreciated provider of jobs and pay-cheques, you mean. Harassed by his ungrateful employees, taken advantage of by greedy customers . . .'

Crysten made a face. 'You're making me cry,' she teased.

Black eyes gleamed at her and, as she turned to climb into her cubicle, she felt a large hand pat her lightly on the bottom.

'Goodnight, witch,' his voice murmured in her ear, as she drew the door closed behind her and began to pull the bed down from the wall.

So I'm a witch, am I? she sniffed, as the bed snapped into place. She climbed on top of it because there was no longer room to stand on the floor. I'll give him witch. But she was smiling to herself as she lay down on the pillow and felt the train pitching and shuddering underneath her.

It was not only the train which kept her awake that night, but the memory of very black eyes and a strong hand which had clasped her own in the swaying darkness of the dome. She could still feel where that hand had touched another part of her body. If only he was beside her now ...

After a long time she did fall asleep, and when she awoke and pushed up the blind, she thought for a moment that during the night the train must have flown her to Fairyland.

In the narrow gap between sill and blind, white flakes drifted softly against snow-covered rocks in a mountain stream. She sat up and pushed the blind to the top of the window. Close at hand there were skidoo marks in the snow and she saw that the train was travelling through an isolated valley ringed by clouds and snow-misted trees. It was still very early and the pink rays of the sun pierced the clouds in places to touch the scene with magic. Crysten caught her breath and thought that she had never seen anything so lovely.

She was still under the spell of the snow when she finally tore herself away from the window and started to get dressed. She changed the black sweater for a pale blue one and decided that the red slacks were still quite neat and wearable. She had no idea whether Gregg, Jake and Jimmy had already gone for breakfast, but in any case she wasn't going to wait for them. There was a faint and tantalising smell of bacon floating down the corridor.

The train was moving quite slowly along the curving mountain track and she reached the dining-car without difficulty. Gregg and Jimmy were there before her, and just as she sat down Jake arrived, clearing his throat and complaining loudly that every time the train stopped in the night he had been woken up.

'Dad's used to planes,' explained Gregg with a grin. 'He likes to get where he's going fast, conclude his business and be back at Mallesons next day.'

'Hm,' grunted Jake. 'Only thing wrong with that scenario is that it applies more to you than to me these days. You may have noticed I don't spend much time at Mallesons any more.' He poured two containers of cream into his coffee. 'And I'd be quite satisfied with this archaic transportation if it would just allow me to get some sleep.'

'I didn't sleep all that well, either,' agreed Crysten sympathetically. 'But it's so beautiful this morning that it doesn't seem to matter.' She gestured at the falling snow and watched a mountain peak, rock-grey in the whiteness, looming tall and lonely above the clouds as the train moved slowly out of the valley.

Gregg, seeing her glowing, delighted face, almost told her that she was far more lovely than the scenery. But in the end he only remarked apologetically that he hoped she didn't mind that they had started breakfast without her.

'Jimmy was up at five a.m. convinced he was about to starve to death,' he explained, directing a smile of parental exasperation at his son.

'That's OK. I might have been asleep, for all you knew,' replied Crysten.

'Fat chance of that,' muttered Jake, but Crysten saw that his mouth had twisted into a grudging smile, and somehow she knew that this cantankerous old man had taken a liking to her. Funny, she liked him too, in spite of his grumbling.

The train was beginning its winding descent into the town of Field now, and Jimmy pointed excitedly at the flat, mud-coloured earth far below them in the valley where the snow had not yet reached.

'Can we get out there, Dad?' he asked. 'I've finished my breakfast.'

Gregg sighed. 'I'm not surprised. You process food the way a tractor eats dirt. Yes, we can get out if the rest of us have finished.' His eyes met Crysten's over the boy's dark head, and they exchanged a smile.

Twenty minutes later, breakfasts dutifully consumed before Field, they were walking in the crisp November air and enjoying the freedom to stroll along the platform without being thrown against a wall or having to force their way through heavy communicating doors.

But the train didn't stop for long, and soon they were climbing back on board as Jimmy informed a grinning porter that trains sure were a neat way to travel.

When Crysten got back to her roomette she found that Jimmy was right behind her.

'But where do you sleep?' he asked. 'There's no room for a bed.'

'Yes, there is. Look.'

She twisted the handle on the wall and pulled the bed across the room.

'Wow!' gasped Jimmy. 'It sure doesn't leave you much space. But it's neat. Real private. I could pretend it was a cave and I was hiding from robbers. Like Ali Baba. Can I sleep in your room tonight, Crysten?'

Crysten blinked. 'Er—well, I'd like to say yes, Jimmy, but where do you think I would sleep?'

'Oh, that's easy. You could sleep with Dad,' replied Jimmy offhandedly.

She heard a sound behind her and turned quickly to find herself staring into black eyes filled with gleeful derision.

'Well, Miss Starr? What about it?' The sensuous mouth was curved in a sexy smile.

Crysten felt the colour sweep across her face, and she lowered her eyes in embarrassment.

'Don't be an idiot,' she muttered.

'Now, Miss Starr . . .' began Gregg, his voice still shaking with laughter. But Jimmy interrupted him.

'Don't worry, Crysten. Dad won't mind. He never minds Aunt Selina sleeping in his room.' Ingenuous brown eyes were fixed on his father's face, which was slowly turning from a dark, attractive tan to a very rare shade of purple.

'Jimmy! What the devil do you mean by that?'

Jimmy was puzzled. 'I just mean it will be fine with you if Crysten . . .'

'That is *not* what I am asking.' The voice, which a moment before had been choking with amusement at Crysten's discomfiture, had deepened several octaves and came out in an indignant growl.

'Oh,' said Jimmy, thinking quickly and beginning to catch on. 'You mean, how do I know about Aunt Selina? Easy. I saw her. Lots of times.'

'You were supposed to be asleep,' said Gregg through gritted teeth.

'But sometimes I have to go to the bathroom,' protested Jimmy in an aggrieved voice. 'Aren't I s'posed to?'

Crysten stole a look at Gregg and saw that the flesh around his wound had turned a livid red. A muscle moved in his throat, and finally he managed to say in a tight, clenched voice that of course Jimmy could go to the bathroom, he hadn't meant that at all, and in any case Aunt Selina wouldn't be sharing his room any more.

Jimmy stared at him. 'Are you mad at me?' he asked at last.

'No, of course not. Get moving now. Go and find Grandpa.'

'And can I sleep in Crysten's room tonight?' Jimmy rarely knew when to cut his losses.

'No!' Gregg's roar reverberated down the corridor and, with a quick, confused glance at his father, the boy scuttled around the corner.

Standing very close to this hunk of seething masculinity, Crysten felt a quick, very physical current leap between them. Their eyes met.

His skin was still angry purple, but the flush she had felt on her own face had completely faded. She tried to control the quiver in her voice as she murmured soothingly, 'He's very young, you know.'

When he continued to stare at her with the look of an outraged tiger who couldn't make up his mind which carcass to devour first, she stepped carefully away from the clenched fists and remarked teasingly, 'Your sins found you out this time, didn't they? Serves you right, you know, for conducting affairs of the heart under your own roof.'

For a moment she thought the tiger was about to pounce. Then gradually the lithe body relaxed, and he leaned his head against the wall. He put his hands in his pockets and surveyed Crysten from under half-closed lids while she stared at the muscles in his neck.

'Hell,' he muttered at last, in a voice from which most

of the rage had evaporated. 'Kids!' He opened his eyes
fully and she saw the beginnings of a smile on his lips.
'You're right, as usual. That kind of affair will be
conducted elsewhere in future. Not that there was much
heart about Selina. Lots of body, though,' he added
reminiscently. His smile broadened. 'I suppose you
wouldn't give serious consideration to Jimmy's excellent
suggestion?' His eyes were very bright, and she felt the
current flare between them again, more compelling this
time. It held them in an electrifying bond that
temporarily robbed her of speech.

Then she shook her head quickly and smiled.

'Not a chance. You promised, remember?'

He sighed and raised his eyebrows in mock despair.
The current faded. 'That was the stupidest promise I ever
made.' The words were spoken lightly, but Crysten had
an odd intuition that he was deadly serious.

Then he laughed and told her he'd see her at lunch.

She must have been mistaken, she decided, as she
watched his broad back disappear round the corner.
Gregg Malleson could not be serious about any woman,
and the sooner she accepted that unpalatable fact the
better.

She spent the next hour in the dome-car. It was full
now, but as the train plunged into a long tunnel she
managed to find a seat next to a pleasant young man
from Australia who told her he was a geography teacher
on a five-month sabbatical in North America.

'I've never seen snow before,' he remarked. 'I can't
believe all this white stuff. It's beautiful.'

'Yes,' said Crysten, staring at grey rocks, perpendicu-
lar under crowns of snow, and the thick white folds
clinging to passing trees like frozen cream. 'I didn't want

to go to Winnipeg because there might be snow. Wasn't I crazy?'

'Yeh,' agreed the Australian, laughing at her. 'Real crazy.' She was laughing with him when she saw a familiar hand grip the rail at the top of the stairs. The rest of Gregg's athletic body followed. He stood beside them, frowning down at the Australian, looking as grim and forbidding as the day she had first seen him standing in front of the jury box.

'Come on, Crysten, I want to talk to you,' he said rudely, ignoring the young teacher.

Crysten pretended not to hear.

'I said, come on,' he ordered, extending a peremptory hand across the Australian's body and taking Crysten by the arm. She jerked it away.

'I'm coming,' she muttered, anxious to avoid a scene. Apologising to her new friend, she edged past him and stumbled down the stairs behind her employer.

'Who do you think you are, ordering me about like your eight-year-old kid?' she flared, when they had passed through the crowded club-car and gained the privacy of the corridor.

She leant against the window and glared furiously up at him.

He bent his head and studied her with an unreadable expression in his eyes.

'Some kid,' he said finally. 'Who was that fellow you were talking to? You seemed to be enjoying yourselves.'

'We were until you came along. And I don't know who he is, apart from the fact that he teaches in Australia.'

'Oh.' The muscles around his mouth relaxed. 'Sorry. I guess I did come across like a bear with bad manners. Forgive me?'

He smiled and raised his arms. Big hands rested on either side of her head. Although he was not actually touching her, she felt like a butterfly pinned against a wall. The magnetic eyes seemed to burn into her soul, which she was beginning to think she would willingly sell to the devil—if his name happened to be Gregg Malleson.

She gripped her hands tightly together and forced herself to return his smile.

'Sure, I forgive you.' She managed to speak lightly, but the thought crossed her mind that this man had only to ask and he could make her forgive him anything.

'Good.' His thumb ran slowly round the rim of her left ear as his eyes held her transfixed. She couldn't have moved had she tried. Nor did she want to. The thumb moved down her neck and rested in the hollow beneath her chin. He was going to kiss her, and she was afraid, yet filled with such longing for him that she was sure he must hear the hammering of her heart.

But the whistle shrieked a warning as the train roared into another tunnel, and in the momentary darkness Crysten heard a muffled oath as Gregg slowly straightened his body, muttering something about stupid promises—and engines.

'What?' breathed Crysten, her pulse gradually returning to normal.

'Engines.' She saw that he was breathing unevenly, but he gave her a rakish grin which made him look much younger. 'I told you I'm nuts about engines.'

He went on to explain that with a mixture of bribery, intimidation and charm he had managed to bludgeon the authorities into letting him take a look at the engine.

'Want to come with me?' he asked. 'There'll be just

time before we hit Lake Louise.'

The kiss that hadn't happened might almost have been a dream.

'Well—not really,' she replied doubtfully. 'Wouldn't it be better to take Jimmy? He'd love it.'

'Are you out of your mind?' He stared at her in feigned alarm. 'You should know my son well enough by now to realise that if we let that little saboteur anywhere near an engine, fire, derailment or head-on collision will almost inevitably follow. No, Jimmy can wait until he's old enough to use his own line of bribery.'

'And intimidation and charm?'

'That, too. Come on.'

Crysten sighed, took a last look at the snow-covered Christmas trees spiking against the sky, and followed Gregg towards the engine.

By the time they reached Lake Louise, she had heard a lot of incomprehensible information about brakes and steering, and Gregg was looking younger every minute as he put both hands on her waist to swing her laughing on to the platform. He held her a fraction longer than necessary, and for a moment there was a strange, startled expression in his eyes as he stared down at the small form huddled in his grasp in a bright green coat buttoned tightly against the icy mountain air.

The snow was featherlight here, and the stop was very brief. They had just time to run along the platform, take a quick look at the engine from the outside and then climb back into the train. Gregg was still buoyed with a youthful enthusiasm for trains which must have been with him since childhood.

Power and noise, thought Crysten, glancing at the strong, virile profile which was gentler and less serious now than she had ever seen it.

But when she next saw Gregg, his face was serious enough to please a judge, and there was nothing gentle about it.

She had returned to her room and was rummaging in her cosmetic bag for a lipstick when she heard a quick knock on the door. Before she could turn round it was open and Gregg's deep voice was demanding curtly if she knew where Jimmy was.

'Jimmy? No, I haven't seen him,' she replied. 'Why? What's the matter?'

'He's missing. Dad says he was with him at Lake Louise and now he's disappeared. I thought he must be with you. But obviously he's not.' He gave an exasperated sigh. 'Your Australian friend tells me he was trying to climb through a window.'

CHAPTER SIX

CRYSTEN could only stare. She noted the faint dilation of
Gregg's nostrils and the deep furrows on his forehead.
The hockey scar was a pulsing, black-seamed wound. But
his eyes, though darker than she had ever seen them,
showed more irritation than real disquiet.

'He was mad at me because I wouldn't take him with
me to see the engine.' Gregg's voice rasped angrily and
boded no good for Jimmy. 'He got off with Dad at Lake
Louise and when they got on again he said he was going
to the dome. Dad said he'd follow in a minute, but when
he did, Jimmy wasn't there.'

'But I don't understand—he's probably just exploring.'

A muscle twitched in Gregg's cheek. 'Sure, *probably*.
But the fact remains that your friend saw a small boy
climbing through a window. So he says. He told him to
get down, and as far as he knows the boy did what he was
told.'

'Then that still doesn't mean . . .'

'No, of course it doesn't. And we're going to find him.
Come on, put that thing down. You take the back of the
train and I'll head forward. I've checked with the porter
already and he's keeping a look out.'

Gregg's tone was not the kind one argued with, but
Crysten, still stunned, did not move.

'I said put that thing down,' he repeated brusquely.

She jumped and realised that the 'thing' he referred to
was the cosmetic bag she had been holding when he burst

into the room. It was still clutched tightly in her hands.

She started to lay it on the seat, but she was not fast enough for him. He grabbed it from her and hurled it on to the floor, seizing her arms as he pulled her out into the corridor.

'Move!' he ordered. Then as an afterthought he added 'please', and gave her a shove that sent her staggering down the swaying corridor. 'And if you see my father, tell him we're not worried. His heart's not good.'

Crysten's heart did not feel good, either, as she worked her way to the back of the train, hammering on every door as she passed. Gregg's high-handed treatment did not bother her this time. He was no longer an autocratic employer demanding instant deference from his staff, but a frustrated parent with a new kind of challenge on his hands. If Jimmy really was in trouble, his best hope of getting out of it lay in his father's talent for getting things done 'now'.

All the same, as she continued to draw blanks with every enquiry she made, she found she was really beginning to worry. Jimmy was a well-intentioned youngster, but full of curiosity and the spirit of adventure—and, as she had once said to his father, he rarely thought before he acted. Though why he should be trying to climb out of a moving train . . .

She didn't finish the thought.

By the time she reached the dome at the back and had found only sympatheic but unhelpful travellers, and one old lady in curlers who was furious at having her sleep disturbed, Crysten's mood was becoming pessimistic. Surely if Jimmy had been found, Gregg would have come to tell her.

As she retraced her steps, still peering hopefully into

empty rooms, Jake Malleson suddenly erupted in front of her.

'Where the hell's my son?' he demanded. 'He said he'd let me know as soon as he found Jimmy.'

'Oh—er—I think they're both up front somewhere,' murmured Crysten evasively.

'Hm.' He peered at her. She could see the lines of worry on his face. 'You're a good girl. Sensible. Just what Gregg needs.' He patted her hand abstractedly. 'But you can't find him, can you?'

Jake Malleson had not founded a construction empire without possessing a healthy degree of intuition. He would be a hard man to fool. Gregg had told her not to worry him, but she didn't see how she could avoid it.

'No,' she admitted. 'I don't think Gregg has found him yet. But of course he will. He can't have fallen out,' she added, more confidently than she felt.

'Oh, can't he?' The old man snorted. 'I raised his father, and he was most certainly capable of falling out.' He stared gloomily out of the window.

As the train pulled into the outskirts of Banff, Gregg found them standing side by side watching the snow make shapes beside the track.

His face was a mask.

'You didn't find him,' said Crysten flatly.

'No.' His mouth twisted. 'And I thought I told you not to worry my father, Crysten.'

Jake swung round, some of his old verve and vigour still evident. 'Don't you talk to her like that, my boy! I asked and she answered. She's a sensible young woman. Some man will be lucky to get her.' He shot his son a look of resigned disgust. 'Provided he's smart enough to know it.' He paused to let that sink in, then added that he'd have Gregg know he wasn't a blithering old dotard yet and he'd thank him to remember it.

For one electric moment Gregg was jolted from his preoccupation and, if she had not been so worried, Crysten would have laughed at the expression of almost comical discomfiture on his face. But the hard, determined look returned almost immediately as he said that he apologised, and was well aware that his father wasn't an old dotard, but right now he hadn't time to discuss it.

'No, you haven't,' snapped the old man. 'Have them stop the train.'

'It's too late. We don't know where or if . . .' He stopped, and the voice that finally emerged through tight lips was granite-hard and controlled. 'We don't know where they ought to look. They'll radio, of course.'

So Gregg was beginning to take his son's disappearance as more than a minor irritation. 'If he is on the train, which he must be,' said Crysten slowly, 'he'll probably get off at Banff. 'I'm getting off, too. I'll check the platform.'

She had to get off. If she stayed much longer in this cramped, air-conditioned conveyance which earlier had seemed so comfortable and relaxing, she would go stark screaming mad.

She turned away from the two Mallesons, who stood immobile watching her walk down the corridor, and returned to the roomette to collect her bag.

As she pushed aside the curtains and started to slide back the door, she found that her progress was halted by a soft obstruction in front of her knees. In her absence, the blinds had been drawn down and at first she couldn't see what had happened. Then, as she grew used to the gloom and fumbled for the light switch, she realised the bed had been pulled out. Now what on earth . . .? She would have to speak to the porter about this next time she saw him.

Then, as light flooded the little room, all thoughts of the porter vanished.

Two pillows and a blanket had been piled at one end of the bed in a kind of barricade, and behind them a small dark head lay against the sheet. Beneath it Jimmy's body was curled in a tight, protective ball with his arm around a threadbare, spotted dog. He was fast asleep.

'Jimmy!' gasped Crysten. 'Oh, Jimmy. What—why— what are you doing in here? We've been so worried!'

Sleepy brown eyes opened slowly. 'Hi, Crysten,' he murmured in a voice still heavy with slumber.

'Jimmy, why are you in here? We've been searching the whole train for you! Your father was going to send a radio message. We thought you'd fallen out.'

'A radio message? About me?' He was wide awake now, and apparently not at all displeased to think he'd been the cause of an emergency.

'Yes. But never mind that now. We've got to find your father. He's still looking for you.'

The pleased look on Jimmy's face disappeared. 'He'll kill me,' he remarked glumly.

'He might,' replied Crysten drily, 'but, as the object of his search was to find you alive, I should think it's unlikely.'

Jimmy digested this hopeful possibility. 'Well, almost kill me,' he conceded.

'Serve you right.' Crysten was unsympathetic. 'What in the world were you doing in my room, anyway? You told your grandfather you'd be in the dome.'

'I was,' he explained as she helped him into the corridor. 'But I bought three cans of pop at Lake Louise and I drank them in the dome and then I had to go to the toilet.'

'I should think so.'

'Mm. I was there a long time.'

'That doesn't surprise me, either.'

'Yes, and when I went back to the dome Grandpa wasn't there, and I couldn't find anyone, so I was trying to look out of the window and some guy with a funny accent told me not to, so I went to see if you were in your room and you weren't, but the stuff from your bag was all over the floor. I picked it up for you.' He paused for breath and looked at her anxiously, waiting for approval.

'Thank you,' said Crysten. 'That was very thoughtful of you.' Especially as it was your father who threw it there in the first place, she thought, resentful now that the crisis was over. 'But I still don't see why you had my bed down and the lights off,' she went on.

The train gave a lurch and a thump as it pulled into Banff and they both staggered slightly. Doors slammed and people shouted, and they had reached the place where she had left Gregg and Jake before Jimmy answered.

'I was in Aladdin's cave,' he explained, as though that made everything clear. 'I didn't think you'd mind. I decided not to be Ali Baba after all, 'cos I figured if I could call up a genie then I'd get to see the engine. You do see, don't you?'

Crysten did, but she wasn't at all sure Gregg would. There was no sign of him now, and he hadn't been in his bedroom when they passed. Neither was Jake in his.

'I expect they got off,' said Crysten. 'They'll still be looking for you.'

'Maybe we should get off, too,' suggested Jimmy apprehensively.

'No. We'll stay right here in the doorway and watch for them to come back.'

'Oh.' Jimmy's response lacked enthusiasm, and he hugged the threadbare dog tightly against his chest.

Five minutes later two tall figures hurried into view. One older and more hesitant, but still walking with an upright, confident bearing, and the other lithe and active with an athlete's unconscious grace.

'There they are.' Jimmy did not sound over-eager.

Crysten began to wave. 'Gregg!' she shouted. 'Gregg! I've found him. He's here.'

Gregg raised his head. A look of enormous relief crossed his face, and it was only when he began to run along the platform towards them that Crysten fully realised just how worried he had been.

Jimmy was swept off his feet as Gregg picked him up, whirled him around his head and then held him easily on his shoulder. His other arm clamped around Crysten's waist and before she knew what was happening, he had lifted her against his chest and was kissing her with slow, deliberate competence in full view of a platform crowded with interested passengers, his newly rescued son, and a father who came up behind them and remarked complacently that it was about time Gregg came to his senses.

Crysten was quite sure she had lost hers. A warm, wonderful glow suffused her as she felt her body respond eagerly to his embrace. She found that she, who had always prided herself on her discretion, did not care one bit that the laughing spectators who surrounded them had burst into a spontaneous round of applause. It was only when Jimmy joined in from above his head that Gregg finally put her down. He stood staring into her eyes with an odd, enigmatic smile on his lips. Crysten had lost the power to speak.

'Hey, Dad!' yelled Jimmy, as the sun broke brightly through the snow-clouds, pushing them aside to reveal a long ribbon of blue. 'Hey, Dad. Are you going to marry Crysten?'

The spell was broken. Gregg's smile faded as he took his arm from her waist and settled Jimmy more securely on his shoulder.

'Are you, Dad?' insisted Jimmy. 'I like Crysten.'

Gregg's face was turned away from her and all she could see was the outline of his jaw, hard and uncompromising against a background of snow-topped mountains.

'I don't think your Dad knows the answer to that one yet, Jimmy,' Jake broke in quietly from behind them. 'He has to ask Crysten first, you know.'

'Well, ask her then, Dad,' said Jimmy, who was still young enough to see everything in basic black and white.

Gregg's jaw tightened. 'I don't think Crysten's interested,' he muttered. 'Come on, Jimmy, the train's going to leave any minute.'

It was true. The platform was empty now and the porter was frantically motioning them up the steps. As the whistle blew and the train moved on to Calgary, Crysten made her way back to her room alone.

She was repairing the chaos of her bed when Gregg appeared briefly to thank her for her help in finding Jimmy and to assure her that he had definitely not murdered his offspring. Apparently Jimmy had been under the impression that Crysten thought Gregg capable of it.

'And aren't you?' she asked, smiling cautiously.

'Probably.' He was equally cautious. 'But apart from the fact that consuming three cans of pop in quick succession is not the sort of thing that deserves a medal for intelligence, I don't think Jimmy did anything I wouldn't have done myself at his age. That's what my father says, anyway—and if it hadn't been for your Australian telling us about a kid climbing up the window, I wouldn't have been concerned at all.' He smiled, but there was something withdrawn about him now and the smile did not reach his eyes. The man who had kissed her with such uninhibited ardour on the platform had disappeared, and in his place was a reserved, wary stranger.

He left almost immediately and she did not see him again until dinner, by which time they were crossing Saskatchewan, and the snow-powdered landscape had given way to long stretches of wild, uninhibited prairie.

Conversation in the dining-car was polite but strained, with Jake doing most of the talking—complaining really, about lack of sleep and trains which wouldn't keep still. Jimmy, who was incapable of keeping quiet even when it was the wisest course of action, was also full of chat and interruptions. But Gregg was silent and introspective. More than ever he reminded Crysten of a tiger about to pounce.

When she awoke the next day, after a night which had been restless, and disturbed by strange, uncomfortable dreams about tigers with deep black eyes, they were only an hour away from Winnipeg. Crysten ate a quick breakfast by herself, threw her clothes back into the holdall, and waited to disembark.

Gazing unseeing at the telegraph posts, small neat houses and tidy greenery of suburban Winnipeg, she relived those moments on the platform at Banff. She remembered sunshine and snow on the mountains and people laughing as Gregg held her in his arms and kissed her with a joyful passion which had surprised and overwhelmed her. She had known for some time that it was not just his powerful masculinity that drew her towards him, although she found that almost impossible to resist. But there was more than that. There was sometimes an emptiness in his eyes, a lonely, self-protective wall which somehow touched her heart. And there had been moments when she had broken through that wall and found the warm, laughing and loving man beneath.

That moment on the platform, for instance—until Jimmy had mentioned marriage. Obviously marriage was the last thing on Gregg's mind. The moment the word was uttered the hole in the wall had been filled in and Gregg had started going on about 'her Australian' again.

Earlier, she had wondered briefly if he could actually be jealous. Now she was sure he wasn't. The only reason he had kissed her was because she had found Jimmy for him. That must have been it. Well, that was fine with her, too. After all, she could never quite forget what he had done to Sally. All she wanted now was to get through the next two weeks and return to her job with Getaway and her carefree life with Raine.

She had reached this point in her reflections when Gregg banged loudly on the door and told her they had arrived in Winnipeg and if she didn't get her act in gear she was likely to find herself in Thunder Bay or Sudbury.

He was right. The houses had disappeared. Across the street towered the green spires of the Fort Garry Hotel. The high roof of Winnipeg Station loomed overhead as the train came to a stop.

She grabbed her baggage, opened the door and ran towards the exit. Gregg was waiting by the step, his hand gripping the rail as he rested on one hip in an attitude of resigned impatience.

'With so little luggage I thought you'd be the first one off the train,' he muttered as he helped her down. 'I guess I was wrong.'

'I guess you were.' Crysten had no intention of explaining that she had been lost in a world of daydreams—especially as most of them were about him.

'OK, now you've mananged to bestir yourself, perhaps we can catch up with the others,' he gibed, taking her arm and hurrying her towards the escalator. Crysten was furious at the flash of response his touch aroused in her body. She saw him glance at her quickly and knew he had felt it, too.

They sped through the station without noting the cream-carved dome arching above their heads, and caught up with Jake and Jimmy, waiting for a taxi on Main Street. One pulled up as soon as they arrived. Jimmy leaped in first. His father reached in and hauled him out again, telling him to learn some manners.

'Sorry,' replied Jimmy cheerfully. 'I was just getting out of the way 'cos I thought you'd want to sit next to Crysten.'

'I'll be very happy next to you, Jimmy,' said Crysten firmly, diving across the seat and settling herself in the corner as she felt the colour rise maddeningly in her cheeks.

Gregg said nothing as he pushed his son ahead of him and settled into the other corner. When Crysten stole a look at him, he was staring straight ahead with no expression whatever on his face. Jake climbed in beside the driver, and a few minutes later they had pulled up in front of a modern chrome and glass hotel a few blocks from Portage Avenue.

Crysten's room was much larger than she had expected, with a wide, clear view of the city. It was not snowing here at all, and there was only a faint white dusting on the streets. Winter had not yet begun in earnest.

She hung her sensible skirts and blouses in the wardrobe beside the sexy red dress, chiding herself again for the aberration which had made her bring it. Then she sank down in an apple-green chair and kicked off her shoes, running her bare toes through the soft pile of the fluffy white rug which covered the centre of a polished pale-gold floor. There was a single red rose in a vase on the dresser, but there was no card with it, so it must have come with the room. She wondered what she would do with the rest of the day. Jake had his eye appointment in the afternoon, and Gregg and Jimmy were taking him there. Gregg's negotiations with Johnson Exteriors were not due to begin until tomorrow.

It was very quiet and cool up here above the city. Crysten laid her head back on the chair and, inexplicably, when she looked at her watch again it was late afternoon. She had missed lunch and was feeling very hungry. Those dreams of black-eyed tigers last night had evidently left her more exhausted than she had realised.

She stood up and padded over to the bathroom. She was splashing water on her face when there was a knock on the door, and when she opened it Gregg stood there, casually attired in a black, crew-necked sweater and a pair of dark grey trousers which fitted him like the skin of some powerful creature of the jungle. Crysten could not control a little gasp. Gregg put his head on one side and gave her a quick, almost knowing smile which was gone as soon as it appeared.

'Won't you come in?' she asked woodenly.

He shook his head. 'No. Thanks, but I promised Jimmy I'd take him for a ride round the city. I've hired a car. Want to come?'

'No. No, thank you. Believe it or not, I just woke up.'

'Hmm.' He studied her thoughtfully. 'In view of the fact that your hair looks as though it's been through the fast dry cycle in a worn-out washing machine, and your blouse is exposing more of your anatomy than is strictly decent—delightful to the eye as it may be . . .'

'What?' Crysten glanced down and saw that it was true. Only one button remained fastened. The bottom one.

'Oh,' she gasped, frantically pushing buttons through all the wrong holes.

Gregg watched her lazily. 'As I was saying, in view of your most alluring appearance, I have no difficulty at all in believing you were asleep.'

'Oh,' she began again, sure that her face must be the colour of geraniums as she realised that her blouse was now done up so that even more of her lacy pink bra was exposed.

'For God's sake, here.' Gregg reached for the blouse, pulled out all the buttons as she stood gazing up at him like a bird cornered by a snake, and in no time flat had all the buttons sedately in place and her blouse tucked neatly into her slacks. His hands were still inside her waistband, cradling her hips. She was sure that he must hear the pounding of her heart, even if he could not see the heat that was spreading like a flame through her body.

Involuntarily she raised her arms. But before they could fold themselves around his neck, he had let her go and stepped abruptly backwards. A maid passing in the hallway stared curiously, and Crysten wondered what she would have made of the scene if she had arrived a few seconds earlier.

'There. Now you're respectable again. Or as respectable as you're likely to be.' A muscle flickered beside the wound in his cheek, but the wary stranger seemed to have disappeared and the teasing, sexy charmer had taken his place—although there was still an odd restraint in his manner.

'I have to go, before Jimmy decides to impersonate a cat-burglar or start a minor riot in the lobby,' he said.

'Yes, of course.' Crysten's cheeks no longer resembled a flowerbed in spring. 'I'll take my own tour of Winnipeg tomorrow.'

'Right. As a matter of fact, the reason I came was to ask if you'll have dinner with me tonight. Dad's orders.'

'I—what do you mean, Dad's orders?' asked Crysten suspiciously.

He rested a hand on the doorway and grinned down at her complacently. 'He says he's eating with Jimmy and having an early night—most unusual for him. So I'm to entertain you.'

'Thanks for the invitation. I can see it comes straight from the heart,' scoffed Crysten. 'You can tell your father

I appreciate his concern, but I'm here to do a job, not to be entertained.'

'Oh, come off it, Star.' Gregg was laughing at her. 'Don't be a fish.'

'A fish?' She was momentarily bewildered.

'Yes. You always rise to the bait—like a suicidal trout.'

'Huh,' Crysten snorted, beginning to laugh too. 'I don't always rise to the bait—and the first time I met you, you said I had a pretty face, and managed to make it sound like an insult. Now you call me a trout.'

'Well, even trout must be attractive to other trout.' He raised a finger and ran it slowly down her nose. 'See you at eight, then. You can wear that red dress. The promising one.'

Before she could tell him she hadn't brought the red dress he had vanished round the corner, and she could hear his feet pounding down the stairs.

She wondered if he ever took elevators.

Wear the red dress, indeed! How did he know she had it with her? And what made him think she had agreed to have dinner with him? To the best of her recollection, she had told him quite definitely that she didn't need to be entertained. He really was an impossibly unpredictable man. After Jimmy's remark about marriage, he had seemed so cold and distant. There was still a certain distance about him, but the ice was undeniably beginning to crack.

She pulled the red dress out of the wardrobe and held it up against her. Yes, it became her very well. It would be a pity not to wear it just to prove Gregg couldn't tell her what to do. She wasn't usually contrary for no reason. Besides, he was quite capable of rummaging in her wardrobe and discovering that she had deliberately ignored his request.

As she lay soaking in the big green bath in order to take her mind off the pangs of hunger, which were very strong now, she reflected that he hadn't actually requested anything. He had *ordered* her to wear it. She sighed. Why was it that she so often found it difficult to do what he wanted? Even when it was what she wanted herself. She supposed it was because she was used to making her own decisions, not having them made for her.

But when she had finished her bath and put on the dress, she had to admit it did something for her. The soft, clinging folds of the skirt hugged the curves of her body, and the low-cut, backless bodice revealed every outline of her gently rounded breasts. Why, she thought with surprise, in this dress I might even rival some of those fashionable beauties I've seen pictured with Gregg.

She brushed her blonde curls and let them fall naturally about her face, applied a little lipstick, pulled on a pair of dark gold sandals and decided she would do quite nicely.

When Gregg arrived an hour later—by which time she had passed the point of wanting to consume a horse and would have settled for a wren's egg instead—it was obvious he shared her opinion about the dress.

'Beautiful,' he murmured, taking her bare shoulders in his hands and revolving her slowly in front of him. 'Quite irresistible. Come on, let's go before I change my mind about seduction before dinner.'

Crysten felt a quick throb of pleasure at his praise, and when she looked up at his tall figure, impeccably clad in a dark suit which made his physical presence even more arresting than usual, she felt a delicious quiver run through her body. If she was irresistible, he was overwhelming. She realised with devastating clarity that if they didn't leave the room right now it was unlikely that either of them would think much about food again that night. What was it Raine had said about rape and her red dress? Just at the moment, the idea had a definite appeal.

'Yes,' she said quickly. 'Do let's go.'

He smiled, a small derisive smile, and she was sure that he had sensed what she was thinking.

The hotel dining-room was decorated in the style of a terraced garden, with wide steps leading down to a shining white dance-floor. The ceiling was very high, with tropical plants reaching towards it up walls of gleaming glass.

The waiter bowed and led them to a secluded table half-way down the terrace, which gave them almost private access to the dance-floor.

'It's very grand, isn't it?' said Crysten, whose escorts had not usually had the money to take her to places like this. Hockey games, movies and nice little bistros in Kitsilano had more often been her lot.

Gregg laughed. 'I suppose it is. Don't you like it?'

'Very much. I could learn to live this way quite easily.' She trailed a finger through the strange-looking vine which hung beside their table.

Her eyes were dancing at him, and he took her hand across the table. 'You don't regard this as sinful luxury?'

She put her head on one side and pursed her lips. 'No,' she decided finally, darting a teasing look at him. 'Not when I'm the one enjoying the luxury.'

'I'm glad you're enjoying it.' His voice was deep and

sincere, and the eyes which met hers were wide, dark and direct. 'You're an unusual woman, Crysten Starr. Most of the women I take out seem to be adding up the cost of the evening to make sure they're getting their money's worth. You're not like that.' He was still holding her hand.

'Why should I be? I was never a genius at maths, and an evening spent with a calculator is not my idea of a fun date.'

'It's not mine, either.'

She pulled thoughtfully at the tablecloth as the waiter arrived with a tall glass of something long and pink. Gregg released her hand. He had ordered Scotch on the rocks, which he downed with startling speed and no visible effect.

'You must be an awfully bad judge of character if you always find women like that,' said Crysten after a while.

He shook his head and his eyes went hard. 'No, I'm a very good judge of character. I have something they want. They have something I want—and I can afford to pay for it.'

'But—I don't understand. You—you must know—I mean, you're not the kind of man who has to buy favours. I think you've always been able to get what you want, haven't you?'

'Not everything.' He leaned back in his chair and his hard eyes challenged her. 'Perhaps I prefer to pay for what I want. That way I know exactly what I'm getting.'

'No illusions?'

'No illusions.'

She nodded. 'I see. No involvement, either.'

'That's right.' His voice was harsh.

'But . . .' She took several quick gulps of the pink

drink. 'You were happily married to Loni. You weren't afraid of involvement then.'

'Afraid? No, I wasn't afraid. I wasn't involved, either.'

She took another gulp of her drink. 'Wh—what did you say?'

His eyes were hooded and she couldn't read his face. 'I said I wasn't involved. I married Loni on the rebound. I thought I loved her, of course—at first. She was kind and good and pretty—and she loved me. She would have been a wonderful mother to Jimmy. But I should never have married her.'

CHAPTER SEVEN

CRYSTEN put down her glass so quickly that it splashed pink all over the table. Gregg ordered another drink for both of them.

'But—why did you marry her, then? Do you mean you were on the rebound from Sally? How could you be? It was you who jilted her.'

'Right.' His voice grated. 'As I said before, some memories are better forgotten.' He brushed a hand through his hair. 'And don't worry about Loni. I was a good husband to her. She never knew how I felt.'

Crysten stared at him and saw that his face had assumed the hard, flintlike mask that so often hid his feelings.

'I'm glad she didn't know,' she replied quietly. 'She must have been a very—trusting—woman.'

He shrugged. 'Why shouldn't she have been? I never gave her cause not to trust me—whatever you may have heard to the contrary. I had no reason to, had I.'

'Hadn't you?'

'No.' The word came out sharply, like the crack of a whip, and the shoulders beneath his jacket were rigid. 'No. I had Loni. I knew she loved me and I—well, why should I make my wife unhappy? The alternative wasn't likely to be any different.'

'It might have been, you know,' said Crysten, appalled at the bleakness in his voice. 'At least—I think so.' She pushed at a curl which wasn't really there. 'And if—if I were married to you, I'd know in a moment if you didn't love me.'

He raised his eyelids and stared at her face with such piercing intensity that she wanted to get up and move away. 'Yes,' he said after along time. 'Yes, I believe you would. But Loni wasn't like you.' He touched his hand briefly to the scar which stood out, black and swollen, on his cheek. 'In fact, she wasn't really very bright.' The words were spoken with a tolerant contempt that made Crysten feel sorry for the long-dead and probably long-suffering Loni. 'Besides,' he was going on, 'it's not your problem, is it? Because you're not married to me.' The bleak look in his eyes had turned to a reserved blandness.

'No,' she replied, forcing a determinedly sunny smile. 'I'm not. Nor likely to be.'

Surprisingly, he smiled back, and she saw his features begin to relax. 'What would you like to eat?' he asked, picking up the gold-lettered menu.

So the door to his past had closed.

'Trout,' she replied pertly, remembering his earlier gibes. 'With almond sauce.'

'Of course.' His smile broadened. 'What else?'

He ordered Chicken Marengo for himself, and when the meal arrived she observed that he had also called for a bottle of Puligny-Montrachet. She quickly finished the last drops of her second pink drink.

'Well,' said Gregg, 'now you know about my lurid past. Tell me about yours.'

'I don't have one.'

'What? No past?' The harshness had gone from his voice again, and it was low, teasing and very seductive.

Crysten giggled. 'Nothing to speak of, anyway. Lots of men friends, nobody serious.'

'No passionate affairs and midnight gropings in the backs of cars?'

'Oh, a few of those, of course. But nothing came of it, I'm happy to say.'

'So am I.' His gaze was warm and affectionate and she had a sudden conviction that he really was glad. But why should he, with his fanatical aversion to involvement, care whether she had a 'past' or not? It didn't make sense. Nothing about Gregg Malleson made sense. She smiled at him, and the smile he gave her back was slow and caressing and incredibly sensual. All she wanted was to touch him, and it didn't matter whether anyone was watching or whether it made sense or not.

Almost as if he had read her thoughts, he held out his hand and asked her to dance.

When she stood up, still hypnotised by his eyes, her head felt peculiarly light and her feet seemed to belong to someone else. But he took her arm and pulled her towards him, and together they floated down the steps and on to the dance-floor. At least, she felt as if she was floating, in a deep, enfolding, wholly sensuous dream. Gregg, on the other hand, appeared as always to have both feet firmly on the ground. But he was holding her very close and smiling down at her with a lazy, intimate awareness.

Quite suddenly, like the light from a rainbow in the strange giddiness of her senses, she understood with almost frightening certainty what perhaps she had known, and resisted, from the moment she had first met him.

She loved this vital, arrogant and totally fascinating man with her whole heart and mind and body. She knew it, not just from the warm, lustful glow which was creeping like a slow-burning flame from her feet to her stomach to the tips of her ears, but from the way she cared about everything that made him Gregg. Once, she had wondered if she would recognise love when it came. Now she knew she would—and had—and nothing could ever be the same again.

She loved his wit and the way he sometimes teased her. She loved his exasperated concern for his son and his direct, though often autocratic approach to his employees. Perhaps most of all, she loved the vulnerability which showed so clearly in his belief that love was an emotion he would never truly know. Someone must once have hurt him very much. As he had hurt Sally.

She flinched away from him as she remembered Sally, but he felt it and pulled her more tightly against him. The music was loud and throbbing and enveloped them in a wild, pounding beat that swept them into a swirling whirlwind of the senses. Sally and everyone else in the room were forgotten as Gregg's arms slid slowly down her back to just below her waist. For a moment his hands rested lightly, then with a little sigh her own arms slipped around his neck and she felt his maleness against her body. Very gently his mouth came down over hers and her lips parted as his tongue explored the yielding moistness within. His mouth became harder, more demanding, and her hands moved inside his jacket, feeling the muscles beneath the smoothness of his shirt.

As the pounding music reached a crescendo, Gregg

gradually released her and reluctantly withdrew his mouth from hers.

'Crysten,' he murmured. 'My freckled evening star.'

She shook her head and the blonde curls danced in front of her eyes. She was slowly returning to earth. She started to speak, but the floor wouldn't keep still.

'Gregg,' she whispered, holding tight to his shoulders. 'Gregg, I think I have to sit down.'

'What is it?' he asked quickly, eyes deepening with concern. 'What have I done now? Aren't you well?'

'I—I'm all right. I just need to sit down.'

But as he led her quickly back to the table, his arm around her waist supporting her up the steps, she was finally beginning to realise that she was not all right at all. She had foolishly, in the heady atmosphere of Gregg's magnetic presence, consumed two highly dubious pink drinks and a considerable quantity of wine on an almost empty stomach. Maybe it was more than just his kiss that was making her head spin in circles.

'Could I have some coffee?' she asked in a small voice.

'Sure.' Gregg gave a signal and the coffee appeared almost immediately.

'What's the matter, Star?' he asked, his eyes fixed sceptically on her drooping head. 'I've kissed you before, but up till now that hasn't caused you to collapse.' He patted her hand and smiled encouragingly.

Now that she was sitting down, Crysten felt better and she managed to return it.

'You do flatter yourself, don't you?' She lifted her head and her eyes mocked him.

'That's better.' He nodded, satisfied. 'That's the Crysten I've come to know and love. Always out to squash my inflated ego.'

She giggled. 'Well, as long as you realise it's inflated . . .'

'Oh, I do.' He raised his eyebrows to the ceiling. 'Even a small dose of your company would remove any illusions I might have had along those lines. And I've had quite a lot of your company lately.' His lips turned up in the teasing smile she knew so well.

'Oh, dear. Am I as deflating as all that?' she asked in dismay.

He laughed. 'No, not really. You should know by now that I don't deflate easily.' He started to rise from the table. 'If you're sure you're all right now, will you excuse me for a minute?'

'Yes, of course.' She watched him as his long legs carried him swiftly down the steps.

She was still staring at the place where his shoulders had disappeared from view when she heard someone clear his throat behind her. She started, and found herself looking into the smiling face of the Australian teacher from the train.

'Hi,' she said in surprise. 'What are you doing here?'

'Same as you, I suppose. I'm staying here. Are you alone?'

'No. No, I'm with my—my employer.'

'Ah! The caveman who hauled you out of the dome that day like a piece of unruly baggage? Lucky for you your hair isn't long enough for him to drag along the ground.'

'He's not that bad,' protested Crysten, laughing.

'No, I'm sure he's not. Would you like to dance?'

'Well, I . .' She looked around, but Gregg was

nowhere in sight. She remembered how she had felt the last time she had stood up, but she seemed to be OK now, and it would be rude to refuse. Besides, he would probably think she was afraid of the caveman if she wouldn't dance with him.

'Thank you,' she replied. 'I'd like to.'

They moved round the floor at a polite distance from each other, and Crysten learned that he was not by himself after all, but travelling with his wife.

'She'll be back in a minute,' he told her. 'Just went to powder her nose.'

'Oh, I see.' Crysten glanced up the terrace and saw that Gregg had returned to the table. His head was thrown back and his eyes were fixed on her with a smouldering, speculative glare.

As soon as the music stopped, Crysten, whose head had started to spin again, thanked her new friend and hurried back to the table. Gregg was no longer there. She looked around and saw that he was now on the dance-floor. The band was playing to a pulsing sensuous beat, and in the centre of the floor Gregg and a leggy, raven-haired beauty in sequinned black were circling each other in slow, rhythmic motions that gave new meaning to the word sex. Crysten watched Gregg's hips move as she had never seen hips move before, in such an exhibition of raw sensuality that she was unable to tear her eyes away. She felt hot tears behind her eyelids and wiped them angrily away. Gregg had a right to dance with whom he pleased—and how he pleased. He had never made her any promises. Just the opposite. The fact that she happened to have fallen in love with him was her problem, not his.

The dance came to an end. Somewhat to her surprise, instead of rushing headlong to the exit in the direction of the nearest bedroom, Gregg escorted the sequinned beauty to her table and strode quickly back to Crysten.

'Well,' he said, standing over her. 'I see you've recovered from your little fainting spell.'

She lifted her chin. 'It wasn't a fainting spell. I just felt dizzy for a minute.'

'But not too dizzy to dance again.' His voice was flat, and quiet.

'No. I'm better now.' She took a deep breath. 'I noticed you decided to dance again, too. I was watching you.'

'Were you now? And what did you think?' The eyes that met hers were hard and dared her to challenge him.

'I thought you were a very good dancer,' she replied calmly. When he did not reply, she added, 'And I think I'd like to go to bed now.'

He raised an eyebrow and, realising how her remark might be interpreted, Crysten felt herself beginning to turn red. But Gregg seemed not to notice.

'Fine,' he agreed. 'Come on, then.'

She was right. He didn't wait for elevators. They walked upstairs in a silence crackling with unspoken invective.

Once, as a scarlet-coated bellboy ran past them with a tray, she stumbled and her head began to revolve disconcertingly. 'Watch it,' barked Gregg, putting an arm around her. 'Let's not precipitate an alcoholic collision on the stairs of one of Winnipeg's most respectable hotels. It won't do your reputation any good. Or mine.'

'I'm not crecipitating an alcoholic pollision,' replied

Crysten with dignity.

'Oh God. You're polluted,' he groaned.

'I am not.'

'A polluted pollision.' Gregg's bad humour appeared to have dissipated, and he started to laugh. Crysten felt a sudden uncontrollable urge to hit him. He had been behaving as if he owned her, and then he'd danced like that with the woman in the black dress—and now he was laughing at her. It was too much. She drew back her arm and slapped him hard across the cheek.

They were outside the door to her room now. He touched his face, a curious question in his eyes. A long red mark flamed down his already scarred face. Crysten gasped and her hand flew to her mouth.

'I—I'm sorry,' she stammered. ' I didn't mean—I didn't think . . .'

'You never do, do you? And *I* don't think I deserved that.'

'No,' she agreed. 'No, you didn't. I really am sorry.' She turned her key in the lock and choked back an unexpected impulse to ask him in. But she need not have bothered. As she opened the door she felt his hands press the small of her back and then slide lower. As she opened her mouth to protest, she realised that the feeling of weakness in her legs had nothing to do with alcohol. In any case, it was too late, because he had already pushed her roughly ahead of him into the room.

He turned on the light and closed the door behind him.

Her legs began to return to normal, and she stared at him. He saw her eyes, startled and anxious, as he took her by the arms and started to move her inexorably towards the bed.

She gasped but, like a hypnotised rabbit, made no attempt to resist. Then suddenly her foot caught in something furry and she stumbled and felt herself falling. She discovered Gregg was falling with her, and then they were both on the floor, wrapped in the folds of what felt like the pelt of some long-dead animal.

She tried to get up, but Gregg's body lay on top of her. As she struggled, his mouth came down hard over hers and his hands started to move urgently from her neck to her breasts and then down further. Crysten stopped struggling and her breathing quickened as her lips began to respond to his. Her body seemed to catch fire and she moved her arms to hold him closer. But just as she felt his hard hands on her thigh and gave a little moan of desire, suddenly something soft and white descended over her eyes.

Desire faded and she pushed frantically at a blanket of dusty fur which seemed to have wrapped itself around her head.

Gregg swore. Crysten choked and tugged at the thing which had trapped them. In an instant the room was garish with light. She blinked.

Gregg stood, breathing heavily, his hands gripping the offending fur—which turned out to be the white pile rug—with his legs apart like some magnificent, avenging hunter. Crysten, staring at him, felt again that wild stirring in her loins. But she said nothing.

Slowly his breathing stilled. He dropped the rug and saw Crysten sitting quietly against the wall. She looked small and vulnerable down there, her wide eyes fixed anxiously on his face. Oh God, what had he almost done?

'I didn't really intend to confirm your opinion that I

was a deranged gorilla,' he murmured. 'I remember you called me that once. I'm sorry. And I suppose we owe this damned white thing a debt of gratitude.' He waved irritably at the rug lying in a dusty heap on the polished floor.

Crysten was not so sure about the gratitude but, as she looked at Gregg, hulking tall and massive against the pale gold wall, his jacket half off his shoulders and the rug now in a humped-up mound at his feet, she felt something stir in her which was only partly desire. It was also a glowing warmth and a feeling of happiness. Her lips parted in a smile. Their eyes met and slowly he began to smile, too. In a minute their smiles had turned to laughter.

Still laughing, Gregg strode across the room and dropped to the floor beside her. He put his arm around her shoulders and they sat side by side, rocking in a paroxysm of shared mirth which lasted until Crysten felt the tears begin to run down her cheeks.

Gregg pulled out a handkerchief and gently wiped her face. She was still laughing as their eyes locked. The handkerchief fell unheeded on the floor and his fingers began to stroke her cheek. Then they moved to the back of her neck and she felt them in her hair, twisting the soft blonde tresses.

Abruptly he pulled her into his arms and held her tight, his cheek resting on the top of her head. His hands were on her bare back, gently stroking her spine.

'I never meant to hurt you, Star,' he murmured.

'You didn't. I was the one who hurt you.' She touched the stitches on his face where the imprint of her hand still lingered. 'I could have opened that whole mess up again.'

'Well, you didn't. I'm having them out first thing tomorrow, anyway.'

'You won't look nearly so wounded and heroic without the scar,' she teased, smiling into his eyes.

He snorted. 'Do I look wounded and heroic, then? And I thought I looked like a refugee from gangland.'

She grinned. 'That, too, but as Jimmy tells me you play hockey every week, I suppose we shouldn't despair.'

'And what's that supposed to mean?' he asked suspiciously.

'Jimmy also says you play too aggressively for your age and that's why you always get hit. So I expect you'll soon look romantic again.'

'Too aggressively for my age?' Gregg exploded. 'Is that what my horrible offspring thinks? I'll have both of you know I'm still in the prime of life, and if either of you doubt it you'll find yourselves with a few romantic scars of your own to prove it—in just the right place.' He moved his hands suggestively down her back.

'I'm terrified,' chuckled Crysten.

'You should be.'

His eyes were staring into hers now, and suddenly the bantering expression faded and became serious. He took his hands from her back and held her gently by the shoulders.

'I'm sorry about the gorilla episode,' he said softly.

'It's all right. I shouldn't have slapped you.'

He looked at her curiously. 'Why did you?'

She stared at the floor and twisted a button on his crumpled shirt.

'If you want the truth, I think it was because of that

woman you were dancing with. And then you laughed at me.'

'I wasn't laughing at you. And you danced with your Australian.'

'Not like that.'

He smiled reminiscently, teasing her. 'No. Not like that. But after all, this was supposed to be strictly a business trip. Not a passionate warm-up to seduction. And if I remember rightly, you made quite a point of it that apart from our business relationship you expected your time to be your own. So I don't see why you should mind how I dance on my own time.' He moved his hands slowly down her arms and the smile he flashed held a challenge.

'Mm,' murmured Crysten, not taking it. 'I'm not sure why I should mind, either. Except that you were supposed to be entertaining me, not the woman in black. And speaking of warm-ups to seduction, what are you doing here? Your partner in that little exhibition is probably down the hall somewhere holding her breath and a good deal else.'

Gregg laughed. 'It's none of your business, my girl, but I expect all she's holding is her boyfriend. Apparently he's an ex-prize-fighter.'

'Ah, I see.' Crysten nodded, regarding him thoughtfully. 'I agree. One scar may be romantic. But a pulverised nose would be overdoing it.'

He made a face. 'Witch! Wouldn't it, though!'

Crysten frowned. Her eyelids were exhibiting an annoying tendency to droop, but before she went to sleep there was something she wanted to know. 'Gregg,' she murmured at last, 'why did you really ask me to come with you? It wasn't just because I have shorthand, was it?'

Gregg shifted away from her and rested his back on the wall. 'I don't know, he replied after a long, uncomfortable pause which made Crysten wish she hadn't asked. 'Sure, I needed help with old Uriah. That was true enough. But you're right.' He grinned suddenly. 'I knew you'd refuse to come, and I wanted to prove I could make you change your mind. I don't like obstacles I can't climb over.'

'Don't you ever walk around them?'

'No, never. Too slow.'

Crysten, watching the confident curve of his lips as he turned his head towards her, felt a sudden urge to shake him. But she found herself yawning instead. Had he danced with the woman in black just to pay her back for dancing with the Australian? If that were the case, he had succeeded. But why should he want to pay her back? He had only taken her to dinner because his father had suggested it.

She yawned again. It was becoming increasingly difficult to concentrate, and her eyelids were very heavy. She felt Gregg's warm breath on her cheek as her head fell against his shoulder.

In the distance she heard his voice saying something about bed, and then she was drifting peacefully away on a cloud of pink-coloured wine.

She opened her eyes. The room was rolling about in a very strange way, so she shut them again.

'Better?' asked Gregg.

'No.' What was he doing in her room? She tried again,

and this time the room stayed still. She was lying in bed wearing nothing but a white slip. Gregg was sitting on the edge of the bed, eyeing her with a concern which turned rapidly to relieved irritation the moment he saw she was conscious.

'Why are you here?' she whispered. 'What time is it? I haven't any clothes on. Did we . . .?' She stopped. Had she missed something?

'No,' Gregg replied. 'We didn't. You were hardly up to it, apart from anything else. All I did was put you to bed. I regret to say.' He sighed.

So she had not missed anything. She wasn't sure whether to be glad or sorry.

'What time is it?' she asked again.

'Two o'clock.'

'Oh, dear. Why are you still here, then? You have a meeting first thing in the morning.'

'So have you, Miss Starr,' he replied with grim satisfaction. 'I've set your alarm for six-thirty. And I'm still here because I wanted to be sure I'll have an assistant in the morning. Now I'm going to get some sleep and you'd better do the same.'

He kissed her lightly on the forehead, slipped the lock into place and closed the door carefully behind him.

Crysten was sure she would stay awake for what remained of the night, brooding over the events of this strange evening. She might be in love with Gregg, but at the moment she wasn't at all sure whether she wanted to kiss him or kick him. In the end it didn't matter, because as soon as he left the room she fell asleep.

'Oh, shut up,' she muttered, as a shrieking cacophony

roused her from a deep, peaceful slumber. She slashed her arm sideways and swore as she heard her brand new travel alarm clock crash to the floor and whirr slowly into silence.

She reached over the side of the bed, picked it up and shook it. Nothing rattled, so perhaps it had survived the attack. She placed it carefully on the bedside table and swung her legs to the floor.

Her head seemed nicely in place this morning. That was a hopeful sign, anyway. She had a quick bath, dressed carefully in a tailored beige suit with a soft, plum-coloured blouse, and rang the bell for room service. She didn't feel like facing a roomful of people yet and, in any case, she wasn't sure what time Gregg would come for her.

He arrived promptly at eight, already minus stitches, and with a neat line all that remained of his scar. His presence radiated confidence and vitality, and he showed no sign that his night had been as short as hers. He was wearing a well cut grey suit which emphasised his powerful figure. If Uriah Johnson found it easy to get the better of this forceful dynamo, he was a better man than she was, thought Crysten as she accompanied Gregg to his hired car.

As it turned out, Uriah Johnson was easily outclassed by Gregg's decisive manner and absolute refusal to be manipulated. He was willing to pay a fair price for Johnson Exteriors, but he was not giving anything away without being one hundred per cent sure what he was getting in return. By the end of the day, the deal was almost concluded and, although Uriah did not look particularly elated, Crysten could see that he was not

dissatisfied, either. Gregg had made a hard bargain but a
fair one, and only a few small details remained to be
cleared up next day. Crysten, who had faithfully
recorded the entire process, much to Uriah's annoyance,
was suitably impressed with her temporary boss's ability.
She was beginning to understand why Gregg had such
an impressive reputation in Vancouver's business
community.

They drove back to the hotel in a tired but satisfied
silence. As they pulled into the car park Gregg asked her
if she had managed to keep up with the proceedings. He
seemed preoccupied, and made no reference to the
events of the previous night.

She told him that she had had no problems with her
notes and would transcribe them for him as soon as she
had bathed and changed.

'Good,' said Gregg. 'I knew you could handle it.'

He gave her a perfunctory smile and added that they
would all be dining together at seven-thirty.

'Don't worry about the transcription until tomorrow,'
he told her. 'It's been a long day.'

Yes, it had been a long day, reflected Crysten as she lay
in the bath, letting the warmth lap over her body and
smooth the weariness from her limbs. But it had gone
well. Gregg was pleased with his dealings with Uriah
Johnson—and he was pleased with Crysten's work, too.
But it was strange that he had suddenly become the
polite, friendly, but withdrawn employer again. A hot
flush stole over her cheeks as a disturbing thought
occurred to her.

What if Gregg was aware of her feelings about him?
It must have shown in her face and her voice and

everything about her last night. After watching him handle Uriah, she knew there was very little that escaped Gregg Malleson's all too observant eyes.

Her face was burning, and she passed a damp hand across it.

Last night, after he had recovered from what he referred to as the 'gorilla episode', he had been so tender and intimate. She knew he found her attractive, that he wanted her. But he had never pretended to want more than her body—which, she noticed, was rapidly acquiring the texture of a wrinkled lobster. She scrambled out of the bath and dried herself quickly. Perhaps Gregg was trying to discourage further intimacy between them because he had spoken the truth when he said he never meant to hurt her—but that was no reason for her to appear at dinner looking like the sort of breakfast even a starving cat would reject.

She smoothed lotion carefully over her body then went to inspect the contents of her wardrobe. Not the red dress tonight, and the only alternative was a flared black and white skirt with the neat black sweater she had worn on the train. She added a thin silver chain and a pair of minute silver ear rings in the shape of shells, and she was ready.

That evening they ate in the hotel's second dining-room, a dim, panelled hide-away with deep red table-cloths over oak, and lighted candles on the tables. Jimmy immediately ran his finger through the flame to prove it wouldn't hurt him, caught his cuff on the candlestick and almost started a fire. It was only Gregg's quick action which prevented their table from going up in smoke. He seized the candlestick as it fell, slammed his hand over the spark which was working its way through Crysten's napkin, and pushed Jimmy's arm out of danger.

'Dear God!' muttered Jake, who had spent the day entertaining Jimmy. 'If I live to see this child grow up it'll be a minor miracle.'

'Huh! If he lives to see himself grow up it will be a major one.' Gregg's voice had an edge to it, and the look he gave his son was not paternal. Crysten noticed a small red mark where his hand had extinguished the spark.

'What he needs is a full-time mother,' declared Jake, looking Gregg squarely in the eye.

'All very well for you, Dad. You wouldn't have to marry her,' he replied shortly. 'And what he needs is a good . . .'

But Jimmy's dark eyes were fixed on his father's face.

'Didn't you like being married to Mom, then?' he asked.

Some of Gregg's soup splashed on to the cloth. Crysten kept her eyes carefully on her plate.

'Yes, of course I did, Jimmy.' Gregg's voice was softer now, and very gentle. 'But, you see, it would be hard to find someone like her again.'

Jimmy was not satisfied. 'But she wouldn't have to be *just* like her, would she? I mean, Crysten . . .'

'Jimmy!' Jake's voice cut in quickly. 'Jimmy, your father doesn't want to talk about it right now.'

The boy's mouth was mutinous. 'But you said I needed a mother . . .' he began.

'I know I did. Now, let's talk about something else.'

Jimmy sighed and subsided, while Gregg continued to drink his soup. Crysten went on concentrating on her plate and none of them talked about anything else at all, until Gregg ordered coffee and suggested Crysten might like to take a tour of Winnipeg next morning as they didn't have to return to Johnson Exteriors until the afternoon.

'I do have some other business to attend to, though,' he informed her, 'so perhaps you would like to take the car. I won't be needing it.'

Crysten thanked him, but said that, as she had not much time, a bus tour might be a better idea.

They parted soon afterwards and Crysten returned to her room. She turned on the television, found herself falling asleep in the middle of a car chase which was supposed to be grippingly dramatic, and decided to go to bed. It had been a short night, a long day and she was very tired.

In the morning as she ran out to the street on her way to catch the bus, she happened to glance back into the lobby. Gregg was standing inside the glass walls, shaking his head at her.

Now what was that all about? she thought a short time later as she leapt aboard the bus and sank breathlessly into her seat.

The tour driver swept his bus briskly through the streets of Winnipeg, pointing out landmarks with a relaxed, easy patter. He gestured at the statue of the Golden Boy perched in gleaming solitude atop the dome of Manitoba's Parliament. But the gleam Crysten saw was the one in Gregg's eye when he had smiled down at her just before he'd kissed her on the dance-floor.

When the bus was unloaded and the passengers were politely shepherded on to the beige-pink marble floor of the Parliament Buildings, in her mind's eye Crysten saw

Gregg in the massive strength of the bronze buffaloes guarding the grandeur of the staircase. In the blue carpeted brightness of the legislative chambers, she saw the blue sky which had stretched above them on a crowded platform in Banff.

In the course of the morning she was shown churches and cathedrals, new, expensive subdivisions and old, historic houses. Eventually, the bus stopped at a dock and she found herself gliding peacefully down the Red River on a small cruise boat. Now she dreamed of sailing in an open boat with Gregg's arm warmly about her waist and the wind rippling through her hair.

But Gregg had become so polite and businesslike again—and if he tried to sail a boat with his arm around anyone in the bracing wind of her imagination, they would certainly end up in the water! She sighed and returned to reality and the bus.

When she walked through the doors to the hotel lobby, Gregg was seated in a leather-backed chair, strumming his fingers impatiently on the arm. Crysten was startled by the instant constriction of her chest. Just the sight of him sprawled in a chair, looking as though he would uncoil into violent action at any moment, was enough to start the blood stirring through her veins.

He glanced at his watch.

'I'm not late,' she said quickly. 'It's only twelve o'clock.'

'If you want lunch, it's not early, either,' he retorted. 'Our meeting starts at one. But I suppose I should be relieved you're here at all.' He shook his head slowly. 'You nearly missed the bus this morning, didn't you? I thought you once told me you were never late.'

'I'm not.' She lifted her chin. 'I caught it, didn't I?'

'Did you? By the seat of your very attractive pants, I suppose.' He smiled and stood up. 'But let's not stand here arguing. There's time to grab a bite before we leave.'

He took her arm and steered her towards the snack counter. She opened her mouth to tell him that in view of the fact she was wearing a particularly sober beige skirt today, there was no way he could possibly know anything about her pants—then she closed it again when it occurred to her that perhaps he *could* know. After all, he was the one who had undressed her the night before last!

She glanced up and saw Gregg's chair twisted towards her. His knees were almost touching hers, and the eyes that gleamed down at her were filled with amused awareness. She decided the subject of her underwear was better left alone.

They ate a quick meal of hamburgers and chips and headed for the offices of Johnson Exteriors. By the end of the afternoon, Crysten's fingers felt as though they had been holding a pencil for a week. But the deal with Uriah had been successfully concluded.

On the way back to the hotel, Gregg asked her if he could look at her notes, promising to return them immediately after dinner.

'Of course,' said Crysten, 'but they won't do you much good. They're in shorthand.'

'I know. But I saw you recording the major points in longhand whenever there was a break in the proceedings. Your efficency impresses me, Miss Starr.'

So she was Miss Starr again. 'My efficiency, but not my punctuality,' she replied drily.

He laughed. 'Ah, but as you told me, you always make

it by the skin of your teeth.'

She refrained from mentioning that it was not the skin of her teeth which had been under discussion earlier, and handed him the notes without a word.

It was only after another meal in the candlelit dining-room, greatly enlivened by Jimmy's account of an afternoon allegedly spent rescuing tourists from bears in Assiniboine Park, that Crysten realised she was ready to start her transcription, but that Gregg still had her notes.

Damn! He was a fine one to talk about punctuality. She rang his room but got no answer. Now what?

She waited another five minutes and rang again. This time the phone did not connect. All right, there was only one thing to do. Beard the devil in his den and pick up the notes for herself.

She slipped her shoes on, straightened her blouse and hurried across the hall.

Gregg's room was one floor up and directly over hers. She hesitated, knocked softly, received no answer and knocked again.

Rats! He was obviously out. Not expecting any result, she turned the handle. Immediately the door swung open, and she almost fell across the threshhold.

There was no one in the room. The trousers from the suit Gregg had been wearing at dinner lay stretched across the bed. On a smaller bed in the corner she saw Jimmy's toy dog abandoned carelessly on a pillow. Odd. If Gregg had gone somewhere with Jimmy, why had he removed his trousers? For a reason she couldn't explain, even to herself, she crossed over to the bed and picked them up. Then, wondering what on earth she was doing, she laid them down again and gently smoothed the creases. The feel of the fine cloth in her fingers gave her a strange sensation of intimacy. She quickly withdrew her hand.

As she straightened, she saw two notebooks lying on the table beside the bed. Her record of today's negotiations. She reached to pick them up, then wondered if Gregg had finished with them. She hesitated. Well, it was too bad if he hadn't. He had hired her to do a job, and she wanted to get on with it for his sake as well as her own. She wished she could do more for him. Of course, there *was* one thing she could do, but she knew that if she allowed that to happen her life would become inextricably bound with his—and in the end she would be the loser.

She tucked the notebooks under her arm and turned to leave the room. But as she passed the dresser a flash of silver caught her eye. She stopped, then realised it was only the light beaming off a metal-framed photograph. The picture inside the frame was of a smiling, brown-haired girl with slightly slanted eyes and wide, curving mouth. It as an attractive face. Not pretty, really. Gregg had said Loni was pretty. Not stopping to think. Crysten took the picture in her hands. In the corner it was autographed. 'To my darling Gregg, with all my love, Loni.'

On second thoughts, perhaps she was quite pretty. Her eyes . . .

A sudden sound made her jump. It came from the corner of the room and was like the damp rub of a body climbing out of the bath. She froze. Was that why Gregg had not answered the phone? Because he had been in the bath? And was Jimmy just down the hall visiting his grandfather?

If Gregg came out of the bathroom now—his clothes were still out here—and in any case he wouldn't like her barging into his room like this . . .

She put the photograph quickly back on the dresser and hurried towards the door. But in her haste she neglected to make sure it was securely balanced, and before she had reached the hallway she heard a loud thump behind her, followed by the sickening sound of breaking glass.

She gasped. Loni's picture had hit the corner of the dresser and its glass lay in chipped fragments on the floor. As she stared, aghast, the door of the bathroom flew open.

'What the hell do you think you're doing?' Gregg's eyes glittered dangerously.

Crysten gulped and took a step backwards.

But it was not his eyes which held her spellbound. Above his waist the bare muscles of his chest gleamed smoothly in the fluorescent glare from the bathroom. His hair was wet and very dark and, silhouetted against the brightness behind him, he looked like some huge, vengeful giant.

He was wearing nothing but a brief, white bathtowel.

CHAPTER EIGHT

CRYSTEN swallowed, her eyes travelling hypnotically down Gregg's lean, tough body to the firm thighs beneath the towel. When she raised her head again she saw that his eyes were still fixed on her in icy accusation.

'Well?' he demanded. 'Satisfied with the inspection? Now, perhaps you'll be good enough to tell me what you're doing in my room? And why my wife's photograph is in pieces on the floor?' His knuckles clenched white on the end of powerful arms held rigidly at his sides, and he took a step towards her. 'I don't suppose it matters to you,' he rasped, 'but his mother's picture means a lot to Jimmy.'

'I . . .' Crysten floundered, 'I'm sorry . . .'

'Sorry I caught you? I don't doubt it. You just couldn't resist the chance to snoop, could you? An empty room and other people's property . . .' His eyes flicked to the bed, where the trousers from his suit lay closer to the wall than he had left them. 'I suppose you've been through my pockets, too. Tell me, was it worth it? Did you find anything interesting?' Behind his anger, Crysten caught a faint echo of some other emotion—some far-reaching shadow of storms long past.

'No,' she cried. 'Stop it! Please.' She was appalled at the violence of his reaction, which seemed totally out of proportion to what she had done. Of course, it *was* his wife's picture she had dropped, but she hadn't meant to, and only the glass was broken.

137

'Please,' she hurried on. 'I only came to pick up my notes. You forgot to give them back. I saw the photo and I picked it up, that's all. I didn't mean to break it . . .'

He was still glowering at her as though she was a particularly loathsome criminal, and suddenly her own temper snapped. Damn it, he had no business to stand there, half-naked, accusing her of petty theft and snooping with intent! Not when she had spent the better part of the last two days doing her best to please him. And not when it had been his fault she didn't have her notes in the first place.

Her face turned very pink and her eyes were as angry as his. 'How dare you accuse me of snooping?' she shouted. 'You were the one who promised to return my notes, you were the one who didn't answer the phone— and you were the idiot who left the door unlocked so I practically fell into your room. I've done my best to do a good job for you. I didn't want to come in the first place. It was *your* idea, not mine. And now it's finished, and I'm taking the next plane home. Goodbye, Mr Malleson.'

She turned on her heel and ran blindly for the door.

But Gregg was quicker. Before she could reach it he had seized her by the shoulders and spun her round to face him. His eyes were still blazing and he was so close that she could smell the warm, soapy scent of his body.

'So it's goodbye, is it?' His voice sliced through her like a knife, cold, callous and wounding. 'All right, if that's how you want it, take the next plane home. I'll see you get your money. That's all you're worried about, isn't it?'

She tried to pull away from him. His unclothed body so close to hers, and the deliberate cruelty of his words, were combining to produce a complete disruption of her senses. She no longer knew what she wanted, or what was happening to her. But she had to get away from this man who had so much power to hurt her—and was not hesitating to use it.

As she twisted away from him, his bare arms swept around her body, pinning her so that she couldn't move, and his mouth came down on hers in a hard, bruising kiss.

Even now, when there was no warmth in his lips, only a desire to hurt, Crysten felt a small stirring of response. But he let her go very quickly and as she stumbled into the hall she heard his cutting voice behind her saying very quietly, 'Goodbye, Crysten. That's just so you won't forget me.'

Forget him? She touched her hands to the places where his bare skin had pressed against her body, and she knew that this was one man she would never forget. Not now, not next year, not ever.

It was only when she collapsed on to the bed and lifted her hands to cover her tear-streaked face, that she realised she still had the notebooks clamped tightly under her arm.

As it turned out, the first flight Cyrsten could get a seat on did not leave until noon the following day. But she made a point of staying in her room until the last possible moment, and if Jake Malleson had not taken it upon himself to call on her, she would have left without saying goodbye. She was so distraught and heart-sick after a sleepless night spent repeating that senseless scene in Gregg's room over and over again in her head, that she couldn't face the thought of seeing another Malleson today.

But Jake came to tell her that Gregg had changed his

mind about staying a further week, and that he and Jimmy had already left for Calgary, Portland and Sacramento.

Crysten nodded. 'I see. Thank you for letting me know. I'm leaving at noon myself, but I expect you know that.'

Jake eyed her keenly, and grunted. 'Mm-hm. Gregg said you had decided to leave immediately. Can I persuade you to change your plans and keep an old man company on the train? You look peaky this morning, my dear. A nice, restful journey would do you good.'

Crysten smiled wanly. 'Thank you for asking. But I must get back.'

Jake did not press the matter, but when he said goodbye to her and expressed the hope that he would see her very soon in Vancouver, Crysten had a feeling that his sharp eyes had taken in much more than either she, or Gregg, had intended.

Raine was not home when she let herself into the apartment, but she arrived about half an hour later and stood gaping at Crysten, with her hands on her hips in an attitude of stunned amazement.

'What the hell are you doing here?' she demanded.

Only yesterday Crysten had heard very similar words spoken in quite a different tone of voice, from someone she did not expect to see again.

Suddenly, it was all too much. Last night she had quickly stifled her tears, trying not to let Gregg's anger touch her. But now she knew it was all over, that she would not be seeing him again, and that, in spite of all her efforts to keep her heart intact, she had lost it, irrevocably, to a man who thought she was a prying little busybody.

She turned her face away from Raine and buried it in a cushion.

A long time later, as her shoulders gradually stopped heaving and the tears in her eyes ceased to flow like a stream in full flood, she felt a hand gently patting her arm.

'It's OK, Crys. Don't cry. That cushion won't absorb much more water—and the bastard isn't worth it.'

'He's not a b—bastard,' gulped Crysten, turning a damp, splotchy face to her friend and struggling to sit up. 'And how—how did you know?'

Raine studied her carefully. 'Know what? That he's a bastard? But you just said he wasn't.'

'No. I mean how did you know why I was crying?'

'Because,' said Raine slowly, continuing to pat Crysten's shoulder, 'after living with you for nearly three years, I have seen you laugh a lot, grumble sometimes, even lose your temper once or twice. But I have never seen you cry. It has to be a man. That one you assure me is not a bastard, I suppose.'

Crysten gave her a washed-out smile. 'Yes, you're right. Of course, it's Gregg. And I guess he is a bit of a bastard. But, oh, Raine, I've never felt so awful in my life! Is this what being in love is like? Because if it is, I hope it never happens to me again.'

Raine shook her head. 'I suppose it can be part of it,' she said carefully. 'But not the part that matters. Crysten dear, if this is the real thing for you, don't let him get away. Especially if he's not a bastard,' she added, smiling.

Crysten sniffed. 'I don't think I have any choice,' she muttered. 'He's furious with me.'

'Want to tell me about it?'

Crysten did, in considerable detail. When she had finished, Raine pulled thoughtfully at her long dark hair and stared unseeing at the window.

'What are you thinking?' Crysten asked her at last.

'I'm not sure. He certainly over-reacted. I wonder why.'

'I don't know, but it doesn't matter. He doesn't really care about me. He wanted a temporary assistant with a passably pretty face, who would cater to his whims and feed his self-esteem. That's all. He's an arrogant jerk with a super-sized ego and a lousy temper to boot.'

'Sounds charming. A lucky escape from the sounds of it.' Raine smiled bracingly at her friend and refrained from mentioning that if she knew Crysten, and she knew her very well, her room-mate was much too intelligent to fall for a man who had nothing to offer except arrogance and a lousy disposition.

Crysten spent the next day transcribing the notes which had caused all the trouble, and typing them up on her old Remington portable. She checked the finished product carefully to make sure Gregg could have no possible cause for criticism, folded it into a large brown envelope and sent it by registered mail to Malleson Enterprises.

And with that, she thought, as she left the post office, she was through with the Mallesons for good.

The prospect gave her no particular satisfaction—and she was sorry she would not see Jimmy again. But somehow, at the moment, she seemed to be completely without feeling. No wonder Raine, who was used to an effervescent, sunny-tempered friend, kept looking at her as though she had changed into a turtle overnight.

She was not due back at Getaway for another week,

but she couldn't face the thought of sitting at home in the bleak November weather staring at the four walls of 2A Chaffinch Apartments. She paid a surprise visit to her parents and sister on the day after she had mailed Gregg's report, and the day after that she went back to work.

Mr Jacobsen was pleased to see her, but puzzled by her unexpected return. When he heard Dan and Don teasing her about the new man in her life, and she responded by telling them to 'shut up', he became quite concerned. Not that there as anything he could do about it. Crysten was performing her job with her usual efficiency, but the life and sparkle had gone out of her. Mr Jacobsen began to think that Gregg Malleson was not such a nice young man, after all.

Crysten had been back at work for a week when she returned home one grey, November evening to find she was locked out of her apartment. She was sure she had put the keys in her bag. Roused from her current apathy, she swore under her breath and started to rummage through her pockets. She had just unearthed two pink tissues, a box of matches, three candy wrappers, a jelly bean and—finally—her keys, when an all-too-familiar voice behind her remarked caustically, 'I see you haven't changed since last we met. Still engaged in the eternal hunt for keys, are we?'

Crysten jumped, hit her hand on the doorframe and dropped the keys at his feet.

Gregg's eyes remained fixed on her face as he bent his knees to retrieve them.

'This is becoming a habit,' he sighed, straightening his tall frame and handing her the key-ring.

Crysten reached for her property, but found she

couldn't see it properly because there was an odd mistiness in her eyes.

'Here.' His hand closed around hers for an instant and she felt something hard and metallic. His closeness was interfering with her breathing.

'Thank you,' she managed to mumble, stabbing the key blindly at the lock. Miraculously, it clicked into place immediately.

She had stepped over the sill and put her foot on the bottom step before she realised the door had closed behind her and that Gregg was following her up the stairs.

'Can I come in? Please,' he asked, as she paused outside Number 2A.

'I—why—yes, I suppose so.' Her mind was a muddled riot of conflicting thoughts and feelings, and she hardly knew what she was saying.

Another door closed behind her and she turned to find Gregg leaning against it with his hands in his pockets, and one leg crossed casually over the other. He was wearing a black wool sweater and jeans, and the sheer virility of his appearance hit her like a blow in the stomach.

'Wh—what do you want?' she whispered. Her grey eyes, wide and questioning, met his dark ones, which were studying her from under heavy brows with such concentrated intensity that she thought the heat of her body must have risen several degrees.

He took a hand from his pocket and gestured at the sofa. Then he paused before saying quietly, 'Sit down. I want to talk to you.'

'What about?' She held her breath, but didn't move.

'About—as a matter of fact, about that report of our

meeting in Winnipeg.'

Crysten's breath came out like air from a deflating balloon. Was that really all he wanted? She was sure he had meant to say something quite different.

'What about the report?' she asked in a small, thin voice.

He gestured again, with a touch of impatience. 'I need it, of course.'

'Yes, but—I sent it by registered mail almost a week ago.'

'You did? Well, I haven't received it.' He spoke roughly, and she felt the blood rushing to her face. Did he think she was lying, then?

'I can't help that. I mailed it.' There were spots of bright, pink colour on her cheeks and her eyes sparked angrily.

'OK.' His black-clad shoulders slouched against the door and his eyes were turned away from her. 'I suppose it'll turn up sooner or later.'

'Yes.' She stared at him. He seemed to have lost interest in the report, but he was making no effort to leave.

Suddenly she could bear this no longer. He was so close, and yet he was farther away from her now than he had ever been.

She started to walk towards him, but when she was only a foot away, something in his taut, coiled bearing made her stop, and she stood motionless, staring at him.

She tried to speak, but found that her vocal chords had temporarily ceased to function. When she could move again, she waved him silently to the chair.

He shook his head. 'No, I'd rather stand. Crysten—I

want to apologise for behaving—like a two-headed bear with the migraine last week. I know it was inexcusable.'

The words seemed dragged out of him, and she had no doubt he found them hard to say. His description of himself was all too accurate, and when she tried to smile her lips froze in an unattractive grimace.

'You see,' Gregg was continuing, 'as I told you once before, you reminded me of someone—of Sally.'

'Yes.' Crysten found her voice. 'The memory who is better forgotten. I wonder if *she* has forgotten.'

For a moment his mouth tightened. 'I assure you, she forgot a very long time ago. In fact, I doubt if there was anything much to remember.' His voice was harsh and contemptuous now, all hesitation gone, and suddenly Crysten's strange paralysis lifted and she backed away from him towards the sofa.

'Oh.' She sat down, shrinking against the cushions and not sure what to say to this unpredictable man who was apologising one minute, and acting like a hard-boiled judge the next.

Gradually the muscles of his jaw relaxed and his features softened. 'I just wanted to tell you,' he said slowly, 'to try to explain—you know I was going to marry her once?'

'Yes, I know that.'

'And when I came out of the bathroom that day, and saw you standing there with Loni's picture broken on the floor—just for a second I thought you were Sally—come back from the past to ruin a perfectly good bath.' He grinned sheepishly, but Crysten could not respond. She knew all too well what this man could do to her if she let him.

'And why should you think that?' she asked quietly.

He shrugged and the grin faded as his eyes fixed absently on a cobweb hanging from the overhead light. 'I don't really know. But she used to do things like that. I'd go into my room at home and find her poking in my cupboards or rearranging the pictures on my dresser.'

'Perhaps she just wanted to know more about you.'

'Perhaps she just wanted to find out the best way to get her hands on my money,' he replied bitterly.

'Is that why you left her? Because you thought that?'

'No.' His voice was low, quiet and very final, and she knew he did not mean to volunteer any more information—but she had to ask anyway.

'If that wasn't why, why *did* you leave her?' His answer was suddenly desperately important.

But it didn't come. 'It doesn't matter why I left her. What *does* matter is that I behaved very badly that night in Winnipeg—and I want you to know I regret it.' He had drawn himself up to his full height now and his body stood straight and rigid against the door, his eyes fixed steadily on her face.

Crysten did not know how to reply to this oddly formal Gregg, but there was no point in refusing his apology, so she flashed a superficial smile and said that of course it didn't matter, and she hoped he would be satisfied with her report of the Winnipeg meeting when it arrived.

Heavy lids closed momentarily over his eyes, and when he lifted them again he just nodded and said he was sure he would be quite satisfied.

For a moment he continued to stare at her as she smiled brightly back.

'Perhaps, if you think you could put up with me, you'll work for me again some day,' he suggested, with a funny, twisted smile on his lips.

She nodded. 'Oh, yes. Perhaps.'

'Well—in that case . . .' He pushed himself away from the door and came towards her. 'In that case, I suppose our business is concluded.' He held out his hand. 'Goodbye, Crysten.'

She took it and felt the familiar jolt run up her arm. 'Goodbye.'

His eyes held hers, then travelled slowly over her face, as though he was trying to fix it in his memory. When he was through with her face, he started on her figure, and by the time he let go of her hand she felt as if her body and everything about her had been laid bare. She started to speak, but before she could say anything he had bent his body towards her, cupped her face in his hands and tilted her mouth up to his. He kissed her with a desperate, probing tenderness and then, before she had time to react, the door had slammed behind him and she could hear his feet running down the stairs. Another door slammed as she dragged herself giddily to her feet and stumbled over to the window. She caught just a glimpse of his hands on the wheel and the dark hair waving on his neck, before the Rover roared into life and shot off down the road as though there were fifty police cars in pursuit—which there soon would be if he kept that up, she thought anxiously.

She could not help being impressed by his driving skill, but she was afraid too. Afraid that he would kill himself if he continued at that speed.

Kill himself. She couldn't bear to think of a world which did not contain Gregg.

She left the window and wandered into the kitchen. Raine was out with Bill tonight, so she was on her own. There was half a cold pork pie left in the fridge. It didn't look very appetising, but it would have to do.

Half of it was in her mouth when John phoned to say he had more tickets to the hockey game, and did she want to go?

She didn't. What she really wanted to do was to sit at home brooding about this latest scene with Gregg. Why had he come here if he was only going to rush off like that, as if all the bats out of hell were after him—along with the Vancouver traffic squad?

Of course, it was true she had barely responded to his apology. She had accepted it and remained politely remote. But what else could he expect? Perhaps if he had stayed longer ... She was afraid to give too much of herself now. He had rejected her before and would probably do so again—given the chance. And, in spite of what he said about Sally's snooping, he was the one who had let his fiancée down. He had not even tried to pretend she had deserted him. No, whatever happened, her only hope of peace and sanity lay in getting Gregg Malleson out of her system—and keeping him out.

'Hey, Crysten! What's up? I said, do you want to come to the hockey game?' John was still on the phone.

She inhaled deeply. 'Sure,' she replied. 'I'd like that very much.'

She was not going to get Gregg out of her system by sitting at home eating cold pork pies. John, with his hockey tickets and broken heart, was just what she needed this evening.

The next few weeks were busier than usual, because Crysten was determined to make a life for herself that did not include Gregg. She took on every extra job that was suggested to her at work, even to running the stamp machine for Don, who was trying to promote the redhead in an office up the street, and wanted to get off early in order to bump into her 'accidentally'.

Crysten's fellow employees were delighted that their always obliging workmate had now become such a pushover for work that they could direct almost any unpleasant job her way. But Mr Jacobsen saw what was going on, and told her that if she didn't let up on the late hours and overwork she would end up in the hospital, and in future she was to leave no later than six o'clock.

After that she concentrated on her life outside the office. John and his tickets were good for several evenings, until it occurred to her that he was beginning to think she had more in mind than hockey. At that point, she told him to find other friends to take with him to the games.

Roger from Sales thought he had scored a coup when she agreed to go out with him again. He took her to a charity ball at the Hotel Vancouver, which was a switch from the dim and crowded night-clubs he usually favoured, but as those had not worked with Crysten before, he hoped the more sophisticated ballroom might produce a more satisfactory aftermath.

In fact, it produced no aftermath at all, because on the other side of the room Crysten caught a glimpse of dark hair curling at the base of a well-remembered neck. The neck was bent towards a tall, willowy brunette with flashing eyes and a seductive smile.

Gregg was not holding her very close, but when he glanced up and saw Crysten watching him, a spasm flickered across his face, and he pulled his partner hard against his chest and buried his face in her hair. Crysten told Roger she was terribly sorry, but she had a blinding headache and really must go home.

The next day Roger turned his attentions to Linda from Accounting, and at five o'clock Crysten found herself sitting at an empty desk with an equally empty evening stretching ahead of her.

She picked up the phone to call her mother—and found that she was dialling the number of Malleson Enterprises instead. When Sheila's voice answered, she slowly replaced the receiver.

What could she possibly be thinking of? She had nothing to discuss with Gregg, and she had long ago decided that her life would be infinitely happier without him. Happier? More peaceful, at least.

And since when has peace and quiet been the height of your ambition, Crysten Starr? she asked herself sternly. The answer, of course, was that until she had met Gregg, peace and quiet had been the last things on her mind, way down the agenda. Challenge, fun and laughter were much more her style.

She sighed and pushed irritably at her telephone directory. It snapped open at the Ms. On second thoughts, she *did* have something to discuss with Gregg. She ought to be sure that the transcription she had sent by registered mail had actually been delivered.

She dialled his number again, but this time there was no answer. Sheila and the new receptionist must have gone home, which meant that if she wanted to talk to Gregg she would have to call his house.

She hesitated. Well, why not? It was only good business practice to make sure that her work had found its mark. She reached for the receiver.

A high, boyish voice answered, and Crysten almost hung up. Then she realised it was Jimmy.

'Is that you, Crysten?' he asked. The pleasure in his voice brought unexpected tears to her eyes.

'Yes, it's me. How are you? How's school?'

'Great. Cassandra Zinger has invited me to her party. And I'm helping her build a new model theatre.'

'That's wonderful. And how's Mrs Mikelchuk?'

'Her hands are OK now—but she says me and Mike better not bring anything to Show and Tell till next year.'

'Oh, I see. And will she be your teacher next year?'

'Nope. That'll be Miss Tilson. Mrs Mikelchuk says me and Mike are somebody else's turn. But I don't see how we can be turn, do you?'

Crysten did, but she didn't think she could explain it to Jimmy—at least, not for a few years yet. And in a few years Jimmy would not be part of her life.

As if he had read her thoughts, he did not wait for an answer, but rushed on, 'Are you coming to see us soon, Crysten? Dad wants you to.'

'He—does . . .?' Crysten was beginning to reply. Then she heard a commotion at the other end of the line, a man swearing impressively, and finally Jimmy muttering aggrievedly, 'Well, you *said* you liked her.'

A moment later, a deep voice which made her catch her breath said quietly, 'Hello, Crysten. What the hell—I mean, is there something I can do for you?'

For a heart-stopping moment she was unable to speak.

'Well? Are you there?' His tone was impatient, but there was a shade of something else—something that was almost—pain?

'Yes. Yes, I'm here.'

She heard his breath, slowly released.

'What is it, then?'

'What is it? Oh, I see. Nothing serious. I just wanted to

be sure that report arrived all right. I couldn't get an answer at your office.'

'I'm not surprised, if you called at this hour. I just got home myself.' The words were flat, unemphatic, and she tried to visualise him standing in the polished hallway, holding the phone in one hand and probably leaning his shoulder against the panelling.

'Did you get the report?' she repeated.

'The report? Sure. It came. Nice job, Miss Starr. Thank you.'

'You're welcome.' She felt like a fool sitting here, fidgeting with a letter opener and trying to prolong a senseless conversation with a man who most likely wanted only to change out of his working clothes and pour himself a stiff drink.

'I'm glad it arrived,' she said quickly. 'I won't keep you, then. Goodbye—Gregg.'

Just as she hung up, she thought she heard him saying urgently, 'Star—wait a minute.' But when she put the receiver back against her ear, all she heard was the steady buzz of a disengaged line.

Damn, thought Crysten. Damn, damn, damn! She should have known better. She *had* known perfectly well that just hearing Gregg's voice again would be more than enough to set her heart and body crying out for him. That had never really stopped—and deep down she was afraid it never would. And hearing Jimmy, too—he had said his father wanted to see her, but Gregg hadn't sounded as if he did—and he had been with that brunette at the dance.

She shook her head, kicked despondently at a waste-paper basket and decided she might as well go home. Perhaps Raine could include her in her plans for the evening because, just at the moment, she didn't think she could stand her own company.

As it turned out, Raine and Bill were going to a party and were happy to take her along. There was a fresh-faced young man there who at first seemed quite interested in Crysten. But when he received nothing but 'mm' and 'I suppose so' in response to his efforts at conversation, he turned his attention to an Amazon from Oregon instead.

On Saturday morning, when Crysten wandered list-lessly into the kitchen in pursuit of toast which she didn't feel like eating and coffee which she had drunk too much of already, she saw that a wintry sun was tinting the grey folds of cloud billowing across the sky. It looked cold outside, but there was a small breeze lifting the branches of the trees. Perhaps it would blow the clouds away.

The day stretched ahead of her with nothing planned until the evening when she was supposed to go to another party with Raine and Bill. For the last few days Raine had been producing men like rabbits from a magician's hat, all lined up for Crysten's seal of approval. Unfortunately, in Crysten's opinion, rabbits—or wolves—were precisely what most of them were. But still she had a desperate need to keep occupied, so she went on falling in with Raine's abortive schemes.

Now she stared glumly at the bare, leafless trees across the road and decided that weather or no weather, she had to get out of the apartment. Washing, ironing and all those boring Saturday chores would have to wait until later.

She phoned her sister, Joy, to try to persuade her to come for a walk in Stanley Park, but Joy only snorted, and reacted as if Crysten had gone mad. 'Take Raine on your ramble through the rain,' she chuckled.

'Very funny,' replied Crysten, giving up all thought of her sister's company. Raine and Bill had gone off to visit his parents, so in the end Crysten set off by herself. Anything was better than brooding in the apartment.

The downtown shops were all sparkling with Christmas glitter, but as Crysten slunk past them in her grey winter coat, she reflected that this was the first year she could remember when the spirit of Christmas had failed to infect her at all. The season of peace and good cheer found no answering cheer in her heart.

But the pale, wet drizzle which fell as she ploughed her way along the sea wall exactly matched her mood. By the time she got home in the late afternoon, she was chilled, wet and even more miserable than when she had started out.

But when she looked up at the door of Chaffinch Apartments, quite suddenly she stopped thinking about herself, and her orgy of self-pity vanished in a wave of concern.

Crouched forlornly in a rhododendron bush by the steps was a small, wet and very familiar figure.

'Jimmy?' she whispered, as something about the way he held his head brought a sudden lump to her throat. 'Jimmy, what on earth are you doing in that bush?'

CHAPTER NINE

THE figure in the bush didn't answer, and Crysten held out her hands. 'Come on, friend,' she urged. 'It's all right. You can tell me what you're doing here after we've got you warmed up.'

Without a word, Jimmy put his hand in hers and stood beside her on the steps as she unlocked the door and led him up to her apartment.

Fifteen minutes later he was curled in a red plaid blanket on the sofa, with his hands wrapped round a big mug of hot chocolate. A smudge of chocolate ran beguilingly across his nose.

'OK, Jimmy,' said Crysten when she was quite sure he was warm, dry and in no danger of imminent pneumonia. 'What's this all about, then?'

Jimmy kicked at a cushion. 'You won't tell Dad, will you?'

'But Jimmy—your Dad will be worried about you.'

'No, he won't. He doesn't like me any more.'

Vaguely Crysten remembered having had this conversation before. But that time the subject had been pyromania.

'Of course he likes you.' She insisted. 'Jimmy, whatever has happened, your father is the person you should be talking to, not me.'

'But he's out. He's always out now, ever since we got back from Winnipeg. And when he's home he doesn't

156

like me. I don't think he likes anyone any more. Not even Grandpa.'

'Oh, Jimmy! You know that's not true.'

'But it is. I heard him telling Grandpa I was a—a public menace and that he was going to send me away—to some school where they wouldn't—wouldn't stand any nonsense, he said.'

'Oh, dear.'

'Then Grandpa said my Dad was a damned fool 'cos he couldn't see the nose in front of his own face when it was plain as a pikestaff to everyone else—and Dad got all quiet and mad and said Grandpa didn't know what he was talking about. What's a pikestaff, Crysten? And I can't see the nose in front of my face, either. Am I s'posed to?'

Crysten smiled and shook her head, bending over to fluff the pillows behind his back so he wouldn't see the tears in her eyes.

'Well, a pike was a pointed weapon that soldiers used to carry,' she replied in a choked voice. 'So I suppose a pikestaff is the handle part. And no, you're not supposed to see your own nose.'

'Why does Grandpa think Dad should, then?'

'I don't know. But, Jimmy, this isn't getting us anywhere. Tell me why you're here. Then I'll see what I can do to help.'

Jimmy shuffled his toes against the arm of the sofa, and stuck a finger in a hole in the fabric. 'Dad was shouting 'cos he couldn't find a clean shirt, and when I told him Mrs Bradford put them all in the wash 'cos he wasn't going in to work today he—he said some words I'm not allowed to say, and told me I was a messenger of doom. So after he left I picked up Mom's picture. *She* wouldn't have called me a messenger of doom.' He sighed heavily. 'But I dropped it and it broke, and I knew Dad would kill me this time 'cos he just got it fixed.' His dark eyes turned to Crysten with a look of hopelessness. 'So I ran away, only I didn't know where to go. And I wished you were there. Then I thought you might be in the phone book and you were, so I took the bus. But you were out.'

He paused for breath and Crysten said gently, 'But Jimmy, your Dad won't be angry with you. Not over a broken picture that belongs to you anyway. He can easily get it fixed again.'

Jimmy shook his head. 'I know. But he'll still kill me.'

Crysten sighed. 'Jimmy, he won't. I promise. Now, why don't you pick up the phone and give him a call? He'll be so pleased to hear from you he'll forget to be mad at all.'

'No, he won't.' Jimmy's lip stuck out obstinately. 'Anyway, he's out.'

'Then he won't even know about the picture yet. But your Grandpa and Mrs Bedford will be home, and they'll want to know where you are, won't they?'

'But they'll tell Dad.'

'Jimmy dear, don't you see that I'll have to tell your father too, if you won't? You wouldn't want him to charge me with abduction, would you?'

'What's abduction?'

'Kidnapping.'

'Wow!' Jimmy grinned suddenly, his eyes lighting up. 'I wouldn't mind you kidnapping me, Crysten.' He stared at the hole in the sofa, which was growing rapidly larger.

'But I guess you're right. The way Dad is now, he might tell the police on you. I think he likes being grouchy.'

'Of course he doesn't.'

But nothing she said could convince Jimmy that his father was not Simon Legree and Attila the Hun rolled into one thoroughly undevoted parent, and in the end it was Crysten who called the house in West Vancouver.

'Thank God for that!' exclaimed Jake Malleson's voice when she explained the reason for her call. 'I'll be right over.'

He was as good as his word. Twenty minutes later a taxi drew up outside, and Jake climbed out of it with an agility which demonstrated to Crysten once again that it took more than the passing of years to slow down the Malleson men.

'Gregg was out when you called,' he explained as soon as he was inside. 'Had to hire a cab. I gave up driving last year, you know. Eyesight got too bad. Where's Jimmy?'

Crysten looked over her shoulder. 'Well,' she said, raising her eyebrows, 'two seconds ago he was sitting on my sofa wrapped in that tartan blanket.'

'Hm. And the sound of my knock on your door was enough to send him scurrying for cover. Not very flattering.'

'No.' Crysten ushered him to the room's only comfortable chair. 'But I don't think it's you he's hiding from. He seems to think your son has homicidal tendencies.'

'Gregg? Hm. I see what Jimmy means, but in fact all my son has managed to exterminate this week has been a piece of his jaw in a hockey game, my favourite forsythia bush when he backed down the driveway too fast, two

perfectly good golf clubs—and rather too many bottles of
Scotch. So far he has shown no signs of wanting to
commit infanticide.' He smiled ruefully. 'For that small
mercy, I suppose I should be thankful.'

Crysten smiled back at the white-haired old gentleman
who sat perched in the chair across from her looking like
an anxious elderly eagle. A wave of affection for him
swept over her.

'I'll find Jimmy,' she said. 'He can't be far away. And
I'm sorry about your forsythia bush.'

'*And* my golf clubs,' grunted Jake. 'Jimmy's quite
right. Gregg hasn't been the easiest person to get along
with lately. He's fired two managers and then rehired
them again, and now he's threatening to fire the new
receptionist.'

'Why's that?'

'Not at all sure. Something ridiculous about her having
too many freckles. What he needs is a good holiday.'

Too many freckles, indeed! Crysten was beginning to
think that from the sound of it, what Gregg needed was a
good kick in the pants—but she doubted if there was
anyone capable of giving it to him. Obviously, she had
made the only possible decision when she had vowed not
to see him again—assuming he even wanted to see her.
Somehow this eminently sensible conclusion gave her
no satisfaction at all.

'Jimmy!' she called. 'Your grandfather's here. Come
on out. He won't bite.'

They heard the sound of a tap running, and a moment
later Jimmy walked out of the bathroom looking as
dignified as it is possible for a small boy to look when he
has chocolate smudged across his nose and a girl's white

sweater tied around his shoulders.

'Hi, Grandpa.' He scuffed a bare toe across the rug. 'I knew you wouldn't bite. Grandpas don't.' He went on scuffing and then his lip began to tremble. 'But I thought you might be my Dad.'

'Oh, Jimmy! Dads don't bite either.' Crysten put her arm quickly around the boy and led him towards his grandfather. 'Come on, let's all have some more hot chocolate and cookies.'

'Cookies? OK.' Jimmy brightened. 'Crysten, are you sure my Dad won't be mad?'

'Of course he won't. Will he, Mr Malleson?'

'Absolutely not.' Jake spoke with conviction. But when a loud, imperative knock sounded on the door a few minutes later, and they heard Gregg's deep voice demanding admittance, Crysten suddenly found she was not very sure of anything any more.

'Hi, Gregg.' She looked up at the tall figure looming in the doorway with his fist raised to knock again, and felt a surge of longing to put her arms around the hardness of his chest and bury her face against the rough tweed of his jacket.

But the expression on his face was not the kind to encourage any such demonstration. He was not looking at Crysten, but staring over her head at Jimmy, who sat wide-eyed on the arm of his grandfather's chair. His jaw was tight, darkened by a faint blue swelling on the left, and his head tilted aggressively. The dark eyes fixed on his son were unreadable.

Jake broke the sudden, strained silence.

'Hah! You found the note I left, then.'

Gregg's eyes shifted slowly to his father. 'Yes. It was on the hall table.'

'I know that. I put it there.' Jake was beginning to sound testy. 'Well, aren't you going to speak to Jimmy?'

Gregg's impassive gaze moved back to his son. 'Hello, Jimmy,' he said in a quiet, toneless voice. 'What did I do to deserve this?'

Jimmy's eyes filled with tears. 'You didn't—didn't do anything,' he choked. 'It was me. I broke my picture of Mom. But I didn't mean to. And I'm really not a—a public menace and a messenger of doom and please, I don't want to go away to that school where there isn't any nonsense, I want to stay home with you.' He gulped, sniffed, made a valiant effort to control the waterworks, and then gave up as two large drops trickled softly down his cheeks.

Turning to Gregg, Crysten saw several expressions chase each other across his face. First a kind of bemused stupefaction, then unwilling amusement, and finally, a gentle, wry regret.

He relaxed his rigid stance by the door and crossed the room in two swift strides, scooped Jimmy up in his arms and pressed him hard against his chest.

'I'm sorry, kid,' he groaned, rubbing his cheek against Jimmy's soft, dark curls. 'Have I really been such an ogre?'

Jimmy pulled his head back and gaped at his father. 'No, Dad,' he replied, amazement in his voice. 'You're not an ogre. I think ogres are s'posed to be even bigger than you are, anyway. But I thought you'd be mad about the picture. You've been mad at lots of things since we came back from Winnipeg.'

'Have I?' His eyes met Crysten's and then moved quickly away. 'Yes, I suppose I have. Tell you what. I'll try not to be mad if you'll try not to break any more pictures or start any more fires. Is it a deal?'

'It's a deal.'

Gregg put him down. They shook hands gravely. The boy's eyes were alight with relief, and the look he gave Gregg was filled with love and admiration.

More than he deserves, thought Crysten sourly. But she knew she didn't mean it, because the look Gregg gave his son was filled with equal tenderness.

'Will I still have to go to that school?' asked Jimmy, apparently determined to cover all bases while his father was still in this surprisingly amenable mood.

'No,' smiled Gregg. 'We'll just have to put up with you at home. Bad luck for Mrs Bedford, isn't it?'

'Mrs Bedford likes me at home,' replied Jimmy with smug conviction.

'Hah! Too true. He's got you there, son.' Jake pushed on the arms of his chair and levered himself up. 'And now that we've got that settled, we had all better get out of Crysten's way and leave her to get ready.'

'Ready?' Gregg's eyes flicked briefly to Crysten.

'Yes, ready,' repeated Jake. 'Her friends will be back pretty soon, and she's just been telling me they're taking her to a party tonight. Knowing women, I'm sure she wants to change out of those slacks into something gay and seductive.' He winked at Crysten and cast a quick, appraising glance at Gregg.

'Right,' muttered Gregg, his face wooden. 'We'll leave you to it then, Crysten. Thanks for your help with Jimmy, and I promise he won't bother you again.'

'He's no bother at all,' she replied indignantly, 'and he's welcome here any time.'

'I hope that goes for me too,' smiled Jake, as he made for the door which Gregg was holding open.

'Of course it does.' She glanced quickly at Gregg, but he made no suggestion that he too might wish to be welcome in her home. It was only as the door closed quietly behind them that she wondered if she had really heard him saying very softly, 'Don't wear the red dress, Star.'

A few minutes later Raine and Bill arrived home, and in the flurry of getting ready for the party, Crysten had no time to think about those surprising, improbable words.

But she didn't wear the red dress. She remembered the last time she had worn it, and she felt again Gregg's hard hands caressing her bare back.

She didn't think she would wear it ever again.

A week later she was sitting on the floor surrounded by mountainous piles of ribbon and paper. She had spent an evening jostling the crowds in the Pacific Centre Mall in order to pick up Christmas gifts for her family and Raine, and she had not enjoyed it as much as in other years. Usually the glitter and the garlands and the atmosphere of anticipation heightened her own feelings of excitement and good will. This year she had found it hard even to care what she bought—until she took herself firmly in hand and decided that just because she couldn't have Gregg Malleson for Christmas, there was no reason to sink into a bog of self-pity and gloom which could only depress everyone around her. Her resolve to carry on as though Gregg had never happened to her was only dented once, when she was looking for a gift for her father and saw a tweed jacket just like the one Gregg had worn the day he came to pick up Jimmy. But she swallowed, took a long breath and passed resolutely on to another department.

Raine had been pleased to see that Crysten seemed to have her old verve and animation back, but every now and then she wondered at the over-bright glitter in her friend's eyes, and the almost hysterical gaiety of her laughter.

Now Raine had gone out, and when the phone rang Crysten was swearing quietly at a bow which resolutely refused to stay stuck to its blue foil package. She gave a last vengeful jab with the tape and picked up the receiver.

'Is that you, Crysten?' asked a voice which should have been familiar.

'Yes, it's me.'

'Ah! Jake Malleson here. Forgotten us already, have you?'

'Oh—Mr Malleson.' Crysten laughed unsteadily. 'No, of course I haven't forgotten. I just didn't expect to hear from you. Er—Merry Christmas.'

'And a Merry Christmas to you, my dear. I hope it will be.'

'Thank you. So do I.'

'Yes—hm—well. Listen, my dear, I know you're probably very busy—time of year and all that—but I was wondering, would you have time to have dinner with an old man? There's something I need to talk to you about. It's important to me, and I think, I hope, it may be important to you too.'

'Sure. Yes. Of course.' Crysten wondered why her head was swirling giddily. 'When did you have in mind?'

'The sooner the better, I think.' He cleared his throat. 'I suppose you couldn't manage tonight? It's Mrs Bedford's day off, and Gregg has taken Jimmy to watch him play hockey.'

Crysten smiled, surprised how glad she was to hear from Gregg's father. 'He's still playing, is he? How's his jaw? Or is it another black eye this time?'

Jake chuckled. 'Jaw's on the mend. No swelling any more. But the way he plays that game I don't doubt he'll manage to break his nose, or lose one of those fine teeth of his before he's through. But never mind that. What about tonight?'

Crysten hesitated. The floor was covered in paper, that obstinate bow had popped off again and rolled underneath a chair, and she had planned to finish her ironing. But what the hell! The chance to see Jake again and to hear about Jimmy—and Gregg—was too good to pass up, and it would be much more fun than fighting recalcitrant bows, or ironing.

'Yes,' she agreed. 'Tonight will be just fine.'

'Splendid. I'll send a taxi for you at seven.'

'Oh, don't worry. I can drive.'

'I've no doubt you can. But as Mrs Bedford is out, and I have no intention of cooking dinner for you myself, I shall be in that taxi, and I'll be taking you to a nice little restaurant I know on this side of the water. So never mind about driving. You just make yourself pretty and I'll be there at seven.'

Crysten was beginning to see from whom Gregg had acquired his domineering ways.

'All right,' she agreed. 'I'll be ready.'

She spent the next hour frantically shoving paper and wrappings under her bed, ironing the yellow linen dress she had bought to cheer herself up, and dabbing make-up at her face in the usual futile attempt to eliminate the freckles on her nose.

At five to seven exactly, she was ready.

When she realised that the 'nice little restaurant' Jake had mentioned was the one she had visited with Gregg on the day they had first met, she almost jumped back into the taxi. But it was already speeding down the road.

It was cold standing in the chill of a damp winter evening. Crysten shivered.

'Come on in, my dear,' urged Jake. 'I don't know why you women spend all day swathed in sweaters like bugs in their cocoons, and then when evening comes around and it gets really cold, you peel everything off and emerge as shivering butterflies. Makes no sense.'

Crysten laughed and found that the warmth of the restuarant was inviting, after all. So what if she had been here with Gregg? At least she knew the food was good. And the memory of Gregg was everywhere. She would never escape that.

'You're right,' she told Jake as he helped her with her coat. 'But I really don't take everything off in the evening.'

'Hm,' he chuckled. 'Just as well, I suppose. I have a reputation to preserve.'

'So have I.'

They were both laughing as the hostess showed them to a secluded table in the corner.

'I hope you don't mind that I didn't reserve a window,'

said Jake. 'Thing is, I wanted to talk to you in private, without too many distractions.'

'No, I don't mind a bit,' replied Crysten fervently. For one horrifying moment she had been afraid they were being conducted to the table she had shared with Gregg. And she didn't think she could have borne that.

'Now then,' said Jake. 'You're looking a little pale, my dear. We'd better order something to put some fire in your cheeks. Filet Mignon, a good full-bodied wine and a nice rib-sticking pudding, that's what you need.'

'It sounds wonderful, but what about my waistline?' yelped Crysten in mock dismay.

'Your waistline is very pretty—as I am not the first man to observe.'

'Oh, thank you.' Now what did he mean by that?

'You're very welcome. Which brings me to the subject I want to talk to you about.'

'Now wait a minute,' she laughed. 'I don't see the connection between my rapidly expanding waistline and . . .'

But what Crysten didn't see was never to be discovered, because at that moment the wine waiter arrived to make a quiet production of opening Jake's full-bodied wine, and after he left, the steaks arrived and Jake started making small talk about the old days in Vancouver when there had been no soaring bridge across the Inlet and the centre of the city did not reach thirty storeys towards the sky.

Crysten was fascinated, but she began to wonder what game Jake could be playing. He had said he wanted to talk about something important, not something of merely historical interest.

When the rib-sticking pudding arrived—a warm, spongy concoction of fruit and jam—she could stand it no longer.

'Mr Malleson, why did you especially want to talk to me?' she asked, interrupting a long reminiscence about pre-war days in the old fishing village of Steveston where he had grown up.

'Ah, yes. I'm afraid I've strayed from the point, haven't I?'

'Oh, it's not that . . .'

'Yes, it is. Truth is—it's hard for me to begin.' He smiled ruefully.

'Well, you started to say that something about my waistline led you to the subject,' prompted Crysten, trying to be helpful.

'Yes. In a way it does, I suppose. But only in the sense that everything about you has a bearing on what I'm trying to say.'

'Mr Malleson, what . . .' Crysten opened her hands, palms upwards, and smiled encouragingly. 'What is it you want to talk about?'

'Not what. Who. My son.'

Crysten felt a rush of blood to her face which was not caused by embarrassment.

'Gregg?' she whispered.

The old man nodded, clearing his throat again and staring uncomfortably at the table. Then he lifted his head.

'Yes, Gregg,' he said firmly. 'You realise he's in love with you, don't you?'

'I—what—no . . .' She stared at Jake, gulped, tried to

say something else and then, to her horror felt her eyes filling with tears.

Jake reached across the table and patted her hand. 'Well, he is. I'm not sure if he knows it himself yet, but I'm beginning to think he does. That's why he was making life hell for everyone else. Like a bear with a sore head.'

'A two-headed bear with migraine,' corrected Crysten with a small smile. 'That's what he called himself.'

'He did, did he? Well, he was right.' He strummed thoughtfully on the table, then glanced keenly at Crysten. 'But he's not acting like a bear now. He's polite, taciturn, very gentle with Jimmy—even more deadly than usual in his business dealings—and totally unapproachable. It's as if all the feeling has been knocked out of him. Sheila says the only time he comes alive at work is when someone suggests buying some new equipment. Then he shouts at them to forget it, and goes back behind his wall.'

'Oh,' said Crysten, trying to imagine a quiet, passion-less Gregg, and finding herself quite unable to do so. 'But Mr Malleson, that doesn't mean he's—in love with me.'

'Oh yes, it does. I know my son. Remember, I've watched him since he was born. There have always been women, hundreds of them. But you're the first one who has really touched him. Even when his wife died, he wasn't like this.'

'But—if you're right,' said Crysten slowly, 'that might be because I'm the only one he couldn't have.' She plucked nervously at the table cloth.

Jake shook his head. 'No. That may have been the challenge at first, although I don't think so. Anway, it's not any more. He's in love with you, and he's suffering torments because he thinks you don't love him.' The old eyes beetled at her from under white brows. 'But that's not true it is? I've watched you too, and I see the same suffering in your lovely grey eyes, don't I, my dear?'

'I . . .' She didn't know how to answer him, and the tears which had been gathering behind her eyelids began to swim down her cheeks.

'Don't cry. There, there.' He patted her hand again. 'We'll have a nice cup of coffee, two or three, if you like, and then we'll talk about it some more.'

By the time they had consumed two large coffees, liberally laced with something fiery, warm and very soothing, Crysten's tears had evaporated, but her head and heart were still spinning with the extraordinary things Jake had told her and she had lost the power to think straight. In fact, she wasn't thinking at all, but she was feeling a very great deal.

'Mr Malleson,' she murmured at last. 'Mr Malleson, if what you say is true, why won't he talk to me? He hasn't been near me for a week—and even then it was only to fetch Jimmy.'

'I don't know the answer to that,' replied Jake, taking another long swig of coffee. 'You'll have to ask him. Perhaps he thinks—that you don't want him. But he'd be wrong about that, wouldn't he?' His glance pierced through the armour she had so carefully constructed, and she nodded.

'Yes. He'd be wrong. But—Mr Malleson, I—I'm afraid. I do love him. Without him everything seems grey and pointless, and so terribly lonely. I'm not used to feeling like that. It's never happened to me before. But—

well—in Winnipeg, Gregg almost seemed to hate me. And there's Sally, too. I know that he walked out on her. I'm not afraid of risks, and loving someone means taking enormous risks, doesn't it? But I'm not sure I could bear it if he walked out on me, too. And the way he acted in Winnipeg when I broke that picture—it seemed that the same thing could happen to me if I let him have my heart. I don't want to love him, you see. But I can't help myself.'

She paused, her eyes widening, for Jake was looking at her with an expression of stunned amazement. And behind the amazement was something else—an almost startled comprehension—and hope.

'Do you mean to tell me,——' he asked after a long, paralysing silence during which they stared at each other with the first faint glimmerings of understanding, 'do you mean to tell me that Gregg hasn't told you about Sally? I thought—I mean you look so like her, I was sure . . .'

'Told me what?' Crysten spoke with an urgency that surprised herself.

He pushed an empty cup away, rested his arms on the table and leaned towards her. The deep, intelligent eyes bored into her as if he wanted to make sure she would absorb every word.

'Gregg didn't jilt Sally,' he said, enunciating very clearly. 'It was the other way around. Sally walked out on him.'

CHAPTER TEN

CRYSTEN tried to speak, found no words came, and reached blindly for her cup. There was nothing in it, and Jake ordered another.

After a long time, a voice which she didn't recognise as her own managed to croak, 'But—my sister knew Sally. She was going to the wedding. She said—she said Sally cried herself to sleep every night for weeks after she lost Gregg.'

'Huh.' Jake frowned. 'If that little gold-digger cried at all, it was because she lost his money, not his love.'

'I don't understand.' Her white, puzzled face stared up at him with a bemused hope.

'Don't altogether understand myself. All I know is he came home one night—he was very young then, only about twenty-one—looking as though he'd been kicked in the teeth. He was very much the worse for whisky. When his mother and I asked what had happened, he wouldn't tell us. But later he did. Said he had gone up to Sally's apartment when the meeting he was supposed to attend that night got cancelled. She wasn't expecting him of course. And of course it's an old story, but he found her—well, I think *"en deshabille"* is the way they used to phrase it in a more genteel age—with a young man Gregg knew slightly from his school days. Forget his name, but I believe he was a medical student at the time.'

'Poor Gregg,' murmured Crysten. 'How horrible for him. But—I still don't understand. Even if Sally did just want his money, why did she jeopardise it like that? And why did everyone say he jilted her?'

Jake shook his head. 'I don't know. But Gregg said we weren't to deny the stories that were going around. He said Sally wanted it that way and he was willing to go along with her. A few months later he married Loni. He was fond of her, I think. But there had been women before Sally, and sometimes I wondered . . .' His voice trailed off, then he shrugged and looked at his watch. 'Never mind. That's all in the past now. In the present we have my son—who is very much in love with you, my dear, and who is going to turn into a hard, lonely, loveless man if you don't do something about it. Will you see him, Crysten?' Jake's eyes were pleading with her, and his hand stretched towards her in a gesture of appeal.

Crysten pulled a tissue from her bag and blew her nose. Now it would be both red *and* freckled. But for once this unattractive prospect didn't matter. Jake had given her more important things to think about.

She picked a crumb off the table and put it absently in her mouth.

'I—I guess so,' she said. 'If you're sure he wants to see me. But please, I do need time. Let me think about it for a while.'

'Of course. But don't think too long, my dear. For your sake, as well as his.'

'I won't,' she promised, giving him a fleeting, almost shy smile.

Jake looked at his watch again and smiled back. 'Time to go, I think. Gregg and Jimmy will be home soon.'

'I'm glad Gregg still manages to enjoy his hockey,' remarked Crysten, making an effort to say something positive.

But Jake only muttered, and said he didn't see why that was any advantage, because Gregg had always played like a madman and now he was playing like a fiend from hell and getting himself thoroughly battered in the process.

A few minutes later they stepped outside to take a taxi home. Funny, it didn't seem as cold out any more.

That night Crysten tossed and turned and tried to think, and all the time Gregg's strong, dark face was there in front of her eyes. She saw him looking at her with that familiar intensity, and sometimes his lips curved in the provocative, sexy smile she knew so well. His absence became an almost physical ache, and she arose in the morning feeling tired, confused and very bad-tempered.

Raine took one look at her friend's blotchy face and the grey bags under her eyes, and remarked that if she didn't stop acting like a turkey, pretty soon she would look more like a gargoyle than a girlfriend.

'And then it will be too late to change your mind, because that gorgeous man won't want you any more,' she finished baldly.

'I'm not being a turkey, and I don't know if he wants me in the first place, and what am I supposed to change my mind about, anyway?' moaned Crysten.

When she saw Raine staring at her, and realised that she sounded exactly like Jimmy, she started to laugh.

'I expect you're right,' she agreed, 'but I'm not sure I can do anything about it.'

'Of course you can,' insisted Raine. 'That's not my bright, indomitable Crys talking.'

But by the middle of the afternoon Crysten was feeling anything but bright and indomitable. The fact was, she felt restless, weary and sick to the stomach all at the same time. When the phone rang and it turned out to be a regular customer complaining that he hadn't phoned up to listen to music while being left on hold, she only just managed to resist hanging up on him. Instead she told him, rather more crisply than was polite, that she had no way of keeping Mr Jacobsen's line clear on the offchance that this particular customer might call, and if he would like to leave a message she would see Mr Jacobsen received it.

When the customer began a long, grumbling dissertation about calls not being returned, Crysten's patience snapped and she put the phone quickly back on the cradle.

Before he could call again, she had picked up her bag, found Mr Jacobsen just finishing his conversation and told him she had probably lost him a customer, and she was very sorry but she had to go home.

Mr Jacobsen took one look at her face and told her to take tomorrow off as well.

But Crysten did not go home. When she put her hands on the wheel of the Honda, it seemed to steer automatically in the direction of Malleson Enterprises.

She walked through the door to the store and the bald-headed man she had met before was again behind the counter. He stuck his head round a glittering Christmas tree and waved her to the warehouse.

'Mr Malleson's probably out back,' he informed her, 'but if not, you'll find him in the office.'

There was a lot of activity in the warehouse, but it was a subdued, wary activity and the men seemed intent on carrying out their jobs with a minimum of conversation. There was none of the easy camaraderie she had observed the last time she was here. And there was no tall figure towering above the others.

As she reached the stairs leading up to the office, Crysten heard a girl's voice saying plaintively, 'It's awfully hot in here, isn't it?'

'It certainly is, Mary.' That was Sheila talking. 'Of course, what we need in this office is an air-conditioning system.'

'What a great idea.'

'Yes, isn't it? Mind you, the only thing is . . .' Sheila paused, then raised her voice. 'The only thing is, I wonder if we've got Mr Malleson's attention.'

From the top of the stairs a lusty voice which made Crysten's body tingle shouted, 'If you're talking about spending money, you haven't got my attention.'

She jumped, caught her foot on the bottom step and landed with her nose half-way up the stairs.

'What the hell was that?' asked Gregg, as the sound of her body hitting the floor percolated upwards.

He didn't sound as though he particularly cared.

Crysten closed her eyes. This was too much. She had come here because she couldn't do anything else, not after what Jake had told her last night. But although she had to find out for herself, she was sure he must have mistaken Gregg's feelings. And now here she was, splayed on the stairs like a day-old calf which hadn't found its legs. It was a lousy beginning to a grand reconciliation scene.

'I sure blew that one,' she muttered under her breath, as she felt strong arms reach under her shoulders.

'You did, didn't you?'

Gregg was staring down at her, and in his eyes was the look she had dreamed of all last night. On his lips was the curved, sexy smile.

She sighed, and he bent down and lifted her easily against his chest. She felt the heat of his body through his shirt and his breath was warm on her cheek. With no effort at all he carried her up the stairs and dumped her unceremoniously in the chair in front of his desk.

'Well?' he said, looking down at her. His eyebrows were raised, and the smile had gone from his lips now. He stood with his hands on his hips and legs slightly apart, in an attitude that was almost threatening. Surely his father must have been wrong. This man was not in love with her.

'Well?' he repeated, as she continued to gaze up at him like a mesmerised mouse. 'What the hell do you think you're doing this time?'

When he spoke he didn't sound threatening at all, only very tired, and behind the tiredness there was a note of quiet resignation.

Hearing that voice, the wall she had erected so carefully around her emotions crumbled instantly to dust. She stood up, and without stopping to think, or even knowing that thought existed any more, she put both her arms around his neck and buried her cheek in the whiteness of his shirt.

For one endless moment he stood absolutely still. Not a muscle moved, and even his heart seemed to have stopped beating. Then with a deep, wrenching groan, he clamped his arms around her waist and hid his face in her hair.

For a long time they stood like that, in an embrace so close that their bodies were moulded into one. His arms moved slowly up her back as he rocked her gently against his chest. Then, after a while, he unclasped one arm to put his hand beneath her chin and raise her face to his.

His kiss was firm, exciting, intoxicating, and as his tongue moved between her lips she tasted a flavour like dry, heady champagne.

'I want you, Star,' he whispered. 'I want you so much.'

As she rested in his arms, and the flames of her own need burned through her body, Crysten knew that she wanted him too. He was holding her with great tenderness and there was no power on earth which could have made her move. He said he wanted her. She had always known that. But . . .

'Gregg,' she murmured, 'Gregg, please . . .'

'What is it?' He was staring at her with startled concern. 'Oh, my God! Did you hurt yourself on those stairs? I never thought . . .'

'No. No, I'm fine.' She laughed breathlessly.

'Then what . . .? Crysten, whatever I've done, I'm sorry. Don't you know that the last thing I ever want to do is hurt you? I love you, Star.'

As his words pierced her heart, Crysten felt happiness surge over her in soft, rolling waves. He had said he loved her, and for a very long time those had been the words she wanted to hear more than anything else.

'You haven't done anything, Gregg, dearest,' she whispered. 'And you haven't hurt me. If you love me, that's the only thing that matters.'

His eyes burned her with a bright, yearning tenderness. 'You love me too, don't you, Star.' It was not a question, but a confident affirmation.

'Of course I do. Oh, Gregg, of course I do! I think I always have. Even before I met you.' She pressed herself against him and ran her finger through the coarseness of his hair.

'That's not possible, my love.' The smile on his lips was

gentle and amused.

'Yes, it is. That's why I never loved anyone before. I was waiting for you.'

His arms tightened around her and in a moment he was kissing her again.

Sheila, holding a document in her hand, looked into Gregg's office for the third time in ten minutes, and remarked that if those two lovebirds didn't manage to disentangle themselves soon, Malleson Enterprises was going to lose an important contract.

Mary, coming to stand beside her, took one look at the lovebirds in question and replied that she didn't think Mr Malleson gave a damn.

Half an hour later Crysten was sitting behind the big desk pretending to read a History of Mallesons. In fact she was staring at a meaningless jumble of letters and dreaming of the strength of Gregg's arms circling her waist. The owner of the arms was storming through the warehouse with lumber, gyproc and a case of bathroom tiles, shouting jovially to his workers that they could all leave early if they would just get this blasted junk loaded by four o'clock.

'After all, it's Christmas,' he announced with a triumphant grin—as if he had invented the occasion himself.

'Hm,' said Sheila, poking her head round the door. 'It's about time you came back into his life, Miss Starr. These last few weeks have been smooth, efficient—and deadly. The atmosphere was so grim I was thinking of retiring early. But just listen to them down there now.' She put her head on one side and followed her own advice. 'Yes, Mallesons has certainly come back to life—and the usual confusion. Perhaps I'll stay after all.'

Crysten smiled her agreement, as from the warehouse which only an hour before had been subdued and silent, came the sound of ribald laughter as someone told a story of doubtful decency. The man who was laughing loudest was the President.

Not long afterwards he came charging up the stairs, swept Crysten into his arms and told Sheila and Mary they could go home because he was shutting up shop.

'Where are we going?' she asked, as he drew her outside and settled her in the Rover. It was very still and cold now, and the promise of snow was in the air.

'Where? I don't know. Somewhere we can talk, first. Somewhere with happy memories. And after that . . .' He gave her the rakish grin that had so bedazzled her in the corridors of the courthouse. 'After that, somewhere where talking won't be necessary.'

'That doesn't sound like my two-headed bear,' replied Crysten, grinning too.

He threw back his head and laughed. 'One head only from now on, I promise.'

The car slid into gear and rolled smoothly along the streets of Vancouver. As the coloured lights and Christmas trees flashed by the window, Crysten wondered how she could ever have thought this season would not be as happy as other years. But of course it wouldn't be. It could only be happier, because this year she had Gregg. Or had she? A little stab of fear grabbed at her. He had not said anything about the future.

Soon he was driving over the bridge which led to the airport. Then the car turned sharply left and swung south. Ten minutes later she peered through the window and saw that they had reached the fishing village of Steveston where Gregg's grandparents had built their home, and which had once been a thriving port and was now a friendly little enclave of shops, restaurants and fishing-boats. It was dark as Gregg drove past the old United Church which was now a colourful bicycle shop, past the Steveston Hotel and up on to the dock. The glow from the dock lights glimmered across the water and as the sound of the car's engine died away the world became quiet, and very peaceful.

Gregg put his arm around her. She rested her head on his shoulder and gave a small sigh of contentment.

They sat like that for a long time before he said briskly, 'Come on, Star. Let's smell the winter on the water and put some colour back in those frozen cheeks.'

'They're not frozen. Just freckled.'

'No, they're not. Your nose is. That's why it's my favourite nose.'

'And I thought you had fallen for my beautiful grey eyes,' exclaimed Crysten with an exaggerated sigh. All the same, she had a feeling that in the very near future she might declare a truce with her much resented freckles.

Gregg pulled her out of the car and held her against the warmth inside his fleece-lined jacket. As they walked beside the water her head rested just below his shoulder and the musky male scent of his body was in her nostrils.

'I thought I'd frightened you away, Star,' he murmured, as they came to a stop where the dock dropped into the Fraser River. 'I thought I'd lost you for good.'

'You had,' replied Crysten with a small sigh. 'I'm not usually such a chicken, but loving you hurt so much, and you seemed so angry and cold in Winnipeg. I thought the only way I could carry on was to block you out of my life.' She lifted her head and looked at his strong profile outlined against the night. 'And of course I thought you had deserted Sally at the last minute, and might do the same to me. Why did you let me believe that?'

He looked away and stared into the water. 'I was very young when that happened. I thought I loved her. When I discovered what a mistake I'd made, and she begged me not to tell everyone because it would make her look like a tramp—which she was——' His mouth tightened. 'Well, I agreed to go along with it. It's hard for a young man to admit to the world that he can't hold on to a woman.'

'Yes, it must be. But all these years later . . .'

He shrugged, his hands gripping the railing. 'I still didn't want to talk about it. And I didn't think it mattered. Besides, Sally has married her doctor now. Why rake up old scandals? He's a successful surgeon in Toronto, I believe, so she has at least some of the money she always wanted.' He lifted his head and his eyes gazed out into the darkness. 'I'm sure if he had been more than a lowly student in those days, she would never have thought of marrying me.'

'I see.' Crysten smiled sympathetically and placed her hand over his. 'And then I broke that picture and everything came crashing in on you again.'

'Just for a moment. After you'd gone I felt guilty as hell. I couldn't face you right away. That's why I took Jimmy and went rushing off on more business. When I got back to Vancouver—and realised it was a hell of a lot more than guilt I was feeling—well, you had disappeared behind some frozen barricade. I thought I'd lost you for ever, Star.'

'For ever?' Crysten's eyes widened. 'No, Gregg. I'm yours for as long as you want me.' She pressed her hands against his chest. His heart was beating very fast and he lifted his big hands and placed them over her small ones.

'I want you for always, Star,' he said, in that deep, warm voice which turned her knees to water.

Crysten closed her eyes as a great rush of tenderness for this man washed over her. She would have given him her love however he wanted it. But the fear that had gnawed at the back of her mind could be laid to rest now. Gregg wanted her for his wife.

She opened her mouth to say 'yes'—and said 'why?' instead.

Gregg closed his eyes. 'Because, my very inconsistent trout, I don't want to spend the rest of my life without you. Don't you know you were supposed to rise instantly to the bait and say "yes", not "why"?'

'Oh!'

'That's not very illuminating, either. Darling Star, for God's sake answer me. I love you. Don't you understand?'

'Yes,' said Crysten.

He groaned and held her away from him, hands gripping her wrists. 'Now what do you mean by . . .' he began. Then he saw that the eyes that were shining up at him were filled with love and laughter.

He made a sound which sounded like an oath and pulled her into his arms.

A light went out on one of the fishing-boats and the water lapped quietly against the dock. But Gregg and Crysten neither saw nor heard.

'When did you know you loved me?' she asked a long time later, as a clean, cold wind lifted her hair. Something soft and white brushed her forehead and when she dusted her hand across her eyes it came away damp.

'I suppose I've always known,' he murmured into her hair, 'from the moment you told me you weren't "open to view" and started walking away from me. I knew I couldn't let you go. Not then. But it took me a long time to accept that what I felt was more than a fleeting passion for a pretty woman. I suppose I had too many bitter memories. Of women who had used me—and of women whom I'd used myself.' He pushed a blonde curl behind her ear and ran his finger down her cheek. 'But it won't be like that with us, Star. I can never let it happen again. Not that way, not with you.'

Another drop of dampness touched the end of her nose. From the safety of Gregg's arms she glanced at the sky.

'It's snowing.' She hadn't even noticed the white lattice carpeting the ground.

'I know. Your hair is all frosted. Like a birthday cake.'

'So's yours.' She saw that the dark eyes gleaming down at her were framed by white crescents where the flakes of snow had settled on his eyebrows.

'I wonder,' said Crysten thoughtfully, lifting her face to the sky, 'I wonder whatever happened to that man with the gentle eyes who attacked his boss with a three-hole punch. If it wasn't for him, we'd never have met. I'm grateful to him, whatever he did.'

'It's all right,' he replied, holding her tightly. 'You can be grateful with a clear conscience. He was acquitted a few weeks ago. Apparently his boss started the fight with the help of an executive ashtray.'

Crysten giggled. 'I'm glad,' she murmured, nestling against him.

'So am I.' He began to lead her towards the car. 'And now that we've settled that, it's time for the second part of our programme.'

'The part where talk won't be necessary?'

'That's right. And I can't have you freezing to death out here. A frozen Star is not part of my agenda.'

Crysten laughed and rested her cheek against the snow-covered fabric of his coat. It felt warm and safe, and as the heat crept softly through her body, she was sure no part of her could ever be frozen again.

It was the afternoon of Christmas Eve. Mr Jacobsen had sent everyone home early and Crysten sat on the floor of her bedroom, attempting to close her suitcase. When she discovered this was unlikely to happen without major reorganisation, she flung the lid back and, muttering under her breath, started throwing sweaters and presents furiously on to the floor.

She and Gregg were going to be married next month, but she was spending this last Christmas with her family. Gregg had promised that he and Jimmy would join her in the afternoon, by which time he hoped Jimmy's excitement might have abated to the point where it would not be courting catastrophe to take him visiting.

She was so engrossed in the impossible task of reducing the contents of her case to packable proportions that she did not hear the rap on the door, and she only became aware of someone's presence in the room when heavy hands covered her eyes and a familiar deep voice told her to 'guess who'.

'Well,' said Crysten consideringly, 'Raine has already left—and the only other person who has a key to this place is Gregg Malleson. So, if you're not Gregg, I'm in trouble—I think.'

'If I'm not Gregg, you bet your life you're in trouble,'

he agreed, swinging her to her feet and pulling her down beside him on the bed.

'That's what you think,' she started to scoff. But a determined voice told her to shut up and close her eyes. When she started to argue Gregg picked up a scarf she had thrown on the floor and tied it gently over her eyes.

'Give me your left hand,' he ordered.

Wondering, Crysten obeyed. She felt something round and smooth slip on to the third finger.

'There,' said Gregg triumphantly, removing the scarf. 'Now you can look.'

She looked. A diamond ring in the shape of a star sparkled up at her in silver flakes of light, its cool, clear brightness catching shining darts from the winter sun.

'Merry Christmas, Star. I couldn't wait until tomorrow.'

Her arms went around his neck and the weight of his body pressed her back against the blankets. 'I can't wait, either,' she murmured.

It was growing dark by the time Gregg raised his head from the pillow. Propping himself on one elbow he smiled his slow, sensuous smile as the fingers of his right hand ran slowly down her thigh.

'Do you think you'll be able to stand it?' he asked, dark eyes teasing.

'Stand what?'

'Living with a retired tycoon, a reformed pyro-maniac . . .'

'And a man who gives me a star for a ring and calls me a beautiful trout? How could I possibly resist?'

*Exciting, adventurous, sensual stories
of love long ago*

On Sale Now:

SATAN'S ANGEL by Kristin James

*Slater was the law in a land that was as wild and untamed
as he was himself, but all that changed when he met
Victoria Stafford. She had been raised to be a lady, but
that didn't mean she had no will of her own. Their search
for her kidnapped cousin brought them together, but they
were too much alike for the course of true love to run
smooth.*

PRIVATE TREATY by Kathleen Eagle

*When Jacob Black Hawk rescued schoolteacher
Carolina Hammond from a furious thunderstorm, he
swept her off her feet in every sense of the word, and she
knew that he was the only man who would ever make her
feel that way. But society had put barriers between them
that only the most powerful and overwhelming love could
overcome . . .*

Look for them wherever Harlequin books are sold.

Temptation™

TEMPTATION WILL BE
EVEN HARDER TO RESIST...

In September, Temptation is presenting a sophisticated new
face to the world. A fresh look that truly brings Harlequin's
most intimate romances into focus.

What's more, all-time favorite authors Barbara Delinsky, Rita
Clay Estrada, Jayne Ann Krentz and Vicki Lewis Thompson
will join forces to help us celebrate. The result? A very special
quartet of Temptations ...

- **Four striking covers**
- **Four stellar authors**
- **Four sensual love stories**
- **Four variations on one spellbinding theme**

All in one great month! Give in to Temptation in September.

Can you keep a secret?

You can keep this one plus 4 free novels